"I think we'd better call it a night,"

Steve murmured. "Kelly-Ann," he tried again, struggling not to get lost in her warmth as she wrapped her arms around him and held on tightly. He felt as though he were burning up inside. What was he doing with her? This woman was a loony pet groomer with a house full of animals, and he was a computer-software creator who lived just across the way. And the fence that separated them divided their lives as well as their life-styles.

"Steve, kiss me again," Kelly-Ann whispered sweetly.

Steve tried to keep his mind on leaving when he looked down into her pretty face. Those green eyes were sparkling like emeralds in the dim light. Her lips had been kissed already until they were full and pouting.

He tried to resist with all his might, but how could he refuse her one more kiss?

Dear Reader:

Welcome to Silhouette Romance—experience the magic of the wonderful world where two people fall in love. Meet heroines who will make you cheer for their happiness and heroes (be they the boy next door or a handsome, mysterious stranger) who will win your heart. Silhouette Romance novels reflect the magic of love—sweeping you away with stories that will make you laugh and cry; heartwarming, poignant stories that will move you time and time again.

In the next few months, we're publishing romances by many of your all-time favorites such as Diana Palmer, Brittany Young, Annette Broadrick and many others. Your response to these authors and other authors in Silhouette Romance has served as a touchstone for us, and we're pleased to bring you more books with Silhouette's distinctive medley of charm, wit and—above all—*romance*.

During 1991, we have many special events planned. Don't miss our WRITTEN IN THE STARS series. Each month in 1991, we're proud to present readers with a book that focuses on the hero—and his astrological sign.

I hope you'll enjoy this book and all of the stories to come. Come home to romance—Silhouette Romance—for always!

Sincerely,

Tara Gavin
Senior Editor

BRENDA TRENT

For Heaven's Sake

Silhouette *Romance*

Published by Silhouette Books New York

America's Publisher of Contemporary Romance

To Libby and Lisa at The Doghouse

SILHOUETTE BOOKS
300 E. 42nd St., New York, N.Y. 10017

BRENDA TRENT,

the author of numerous novels and short stories, is an inveterate traveler who has visited most of the U.S. and much of the world but confesses that the home in Virginia she shares with her pets is her favorite place. Her firm credo is that life is to be lived and love is what makes it viable. Her passions include reading, movies, plays and concerts. But writing, she says, is her biggest passion and truly what makes all the rest of life meaningful.

A Note from the Author

Dear Reader,

I've been writing for Silhouette for ten years and I'm delighted to be included in the WRITTEN IN THE STARS series with a story featuring one of my favorite astrological signs—Pisces. I love the water, and the symbol for Pisces is two fish, pulling in opposite directions. My own sign is Aries, the ram, so we're next to each other on the charts.

An avid romantic, I've always been fascinated by the infinite possiblities of how couples meet and match. What determines destiny? How do lovers cross paths and then how do they know, with so many people in the world, that this is the special person? Who knows when Mr. Right might show up?

Love really is what makes the world go around, and falling in love is so splendid that one dare not miss a single chance—written in the stars or not!

Sincerely,
Brenda Trent

Chapter One

"Good boy," Kelly-Ann crooned softly, meeting the huge, liquid brown eyes of the sopping wet mixed shepherd-sheepdog she was bathing. "Good, good boy."

Horace, the dog, wasn't impressed with her words of praise or her bubbly good cheer. He was trying his best to escape, straining and struggling against the leash that kept him prisoner in the despised bath. Kelly-Ann had been so busy with show dogs that she'd kept Horace overnight, testing what little patience he had by confining him so long.

With her favorite radio station playing a song about new love, she worked quickly and efficiently, lathering the long shaggy fur, constantly reassuring him.

She wasn't aware that Pierre, her assistant, watched with admiration, or that someone had entered the shop until the dogs suddenly wailed, howled and barked in unison.

Leaving Horace with Pierre, Kelly-Ann hurried into the reception area of the pet grooming shop. The customer was banging on the desk bell insistently.

She paused at the café door that led into the reception room and saw a handsome man standing there. He looked like someone caught in a whirling eddy that still had him spinning.

"Is anybody here? Hello!" he called loudly, obviously not seeing Kelly-Ann. He was watching a pale blue parakeet happily chirping in a cage on the perch near the window.

"Get yourself out here, woman!" Still not looking up, he clapped his hands. "Come on! Chop-chop! Move it!"

"Great Scot!" Kelly-Ann muttered to herself. "Who does he think he is?"

Chop-chop? Move it? If he hadn't said woman, she would have been sure he was calling for his pet. Talk about impatient!

Barely suppressing her amusement at his disheveled appearance, Kelly-Ann took a moment to study him. He had tousled curly black hair that definitely hadn't been combed, a half-buttoned shirt that revealed dark chest hair, and a tie haphazardly slung around the collar of his mismatched clothing.

She had the most foolish urge to smooth his unruly hair and fix his tie for him. It wasn't that he was extraordinarily handsome; he just looked unusually appealing with his strong, angular face and full lips.

When she caught the look in his dark eyes, she recalled that he was in a rush. Good grief! She'd better channel her thoughts somewhere other than his good looks.

"Saints above, what on earth is your hurry?" she asked as she came through the swinging café door.

He looked at her, clearly surprised and embarrassed.

"Oh! Hello! I expected Suzette. I was beginning to wonder if the place was deserted except for the animals," he said.

Despite the twinkle in her green eyes, Kelly-Ann declared, "You look like a man riding a lightning bolt. I don't allow cardiac arrest in here—for patrons or pets or pet-shop workers. Please calm down."

When a sheepish smile spread slowly over the man's full lips, Kelly-Ann was the one surprised. She hadn't thought he'd react with less than frantic impatience. Despite being a man on the move, he apparently was uncomfortable causing a commotion.

That was something in his favor. That and the unmistakable fact that he was very attractive in spite of his disorderly appearance.

"Who are you?" he asked.

"Kelly-Ann Keernan."

She knew that despite the name K.K.'s Number Two Pet Perfections, most people thought Suzette Towers owned this shop. Kelly-Ann spent most of her time at the other shop, Number One, near her home.

"I'm Steve Jamison," he said, holding out his hand.

Kelly-Ann watched as his large, warm hand enveloped hers. She routinely shook hands as a gesture of goodwill and because she genuinely liked people, but she found herself thinking that not only was her hand wet, it was rough, no matter how much lotion she used.

Quickly withdrawing dripping fingers, she murmured, "Sorry."

"That's okay. I understand." Steve grinned, but Kelly-Ann noticed that he seemed at a loss as to what to do about his own soapy, wet hand.

At that moment she lacked the presence of mind to offer him a towel. She stood motionless, wishing she'd wiped her hand on her apron before coming out front.

They gazed at each other for one more moment, then he murmured, "Sorry about the ruckus. I don't usually carry on so. Well," he amended, "occasionally I do to be playful, but it doesn't create such commotion."

Grinning impishly, her dimples showing, Kelly-Ann commented, "We don't generally have so many dogs. Everyone is in such a terrible hurry this week, but then, all hurries are terrible, aren't they?"

She knew about being rushed. Her business kept her so busy that she had to make a conscious effort to keep on an even keel.

"Pardon me?" Steve Jamison said.

He couldn't concentrate on what this woman was saying. Her voice was wonderfully...*sweet* was the only word that came to mind. He could imagine her soothing a frightened animal, winning confidence with her warm presence and pleasant voice.

Kelly-Ann wasn't aware that he was looking at her with the same amused tolerance with which she had been studying him until his gaze strayed to the skirt hitched up beneath her apron. She had an eye examination scheduled later on and knew she wouldn't have time to change clothes.

A slight shiver raced over her. She was determined to make an impression on Ted Haffner, her ophthalmologist, so she'd dressed with particular care this morning.

Her horoscope predicted positive interactions today. She meant to be ready. She'd been interested in Ted since high school, and although they dated, he'd remained elusive. She felt she needed to prime the stars a bit. After all, she was twenty-five and had no family left. If she hoped to rear seven children—

"I beg your pardon," the man repeated. "What was that about hurries?"

Hurries! Kelly-Ann blinked. *Hurries!* Here she was daydreaming about babies, and this man was in a hurry. Fanciful flights was a Cancerian trait that got her into a lot of trouble!

"All hurries are terrible," she repeated. "Life is too short for us to race about."

Now it was the man's turn to shake his head. Despite her dimples and honeyed voice, he didn't have time for a life-is-so-short speech.

"Is Suzette in?" he asked, wanting to short-circuit this female if she was going to lecture him.

Kelly-Ann shook her head. "No. How may I help you?"

"I expected Suzette," he said.

Although that had become obvious, Kelly-Ann noted, "She's at the other shop, Number One. It doesn't have the spacious bathing facilities this one has, so once a month Suzette and I switch." She paused. "I always bathe the biggest animals."

Smiling, her green eyes bright, she added, "Suzette says that working with the large dogs makes her back ache."

Kelly-Ann almost added that she didn't mind the big animals. She couldn't keep two shops open without Suzette, who had worked for her for five years and managed the second shop beautifully. When the man glanced around restlessly, Kelly-Ann told herself to keep the idle chatter to a minimum.

"You must think I'm crazy," Steve murmured. "Suzette's used to me, but regardless of why you're here and how much you hate hurries, I *am* in one. This morning is already an hour too short."

"I see."

And she did. He'd barreled in here expecting Suzette to cater to him. The woman had a knack that encouraged each customer to think he or she was special.

"Suzette was supposed to have George Washington Jefferson IV ready by nine," Steve said.

Kelly-Ann assumed her best professional manner. "I'm afraid she didn't mention it to me. There's a dog show in Greensboro and we've been inundated by owners who wanted their animals ready this morning. Many of them only brought them in *yesterday!*"

"Yes," Steve said, shifting his weight from one foot to the other.

He was one of those people who'd left a dog yesterday; he'd had no choice. He detested disorder and disruptions in his life as much as anyone—maybe more. His upbringing in a military family and his education in military schools had instilled in him a need for strict schedules.

"The date had to be changed because of the snow,"
he said. "No one expected it this late in March. I'm in
a *desperate* rush to get to the show myself," he stressed,
considering every second they talked a second lost.

Kelly-Ann raised naturally arched brown eyebrows.
"I suspected that when you beat the ding right out of
the bell. And you didn't quite finish dressing before
you came."

She didn't know what prompted her to call that to his
attention. Of course he knew it. But she couldn't seem
to stop staring. Her gaze was drawn to his long fingers. He had buttoned his shirt and was tying his tie as
he spoke.

"The bell's kind of a game with Suzette," he muttered half-apologetically, feeling foolish. "As I explained, I didn't think I'd disturb so many dogs this
early in the morning."

He looked at her emerald eyes, and following her
gaze, he glanced down at his clothes. "I overslept," he
said a bit defensively.

He definitely didn't like flying in here helter-skelter,
half-dressed. He hated to conduct himself that way. He
was ill at ease with this show-dog stuff anyway, and
wasn't used to having an animal around, much less
letting one dictate his schedule.

He wanted to bemoan his goodwill gesture in giving
the dog to his younger sister, Carlene. If he'd had any
idea what he'd been getting into...

He should have had some idea, he reminded himself. After all, there was that crazy woman right in his
own neighborhood who had a yard full of barking dogs
and yowling cats. She'd been trouble from the moment he bought the condominium.

He exhaled tiredly. He didn't know why he was thinking of her now; he supposed it was because of the noisy dogs here in the grooming shop. He glanced around and guessed the room was as orderly as it could be, considering what the business was.

He'd discovered that a single dog could create havoc if it chose to. But that was after the fact. He'd agreed to allow his sister, Carlene, to use his place as a home base. When their father's job required a move overseas, sixteen-year-old Carlene had pleaded to be allowed to finish high school at her boarding school.

After she broke both her legs in a skiing accident several weeks later, she was moved to Steve's home to recover. Abruptly, he found himself getting a crash course in adolescent care.

It was a *gross* understatement to say his life-style was altered by the moody, immobilized teenager whom he adored, but by virtue of age difference, had had limited contact with.

In desperation, he'd gotten her the purebred collie for company. His universe instantly spun out of control as Carlene vicariously threw herself into the world of dog shows: Steve was the door through which she entered, whether he wanted to be or not.

It wasn't that he didn't like Jeffy or love Carlene; it was just that the dog, like the teenager, was more than he'd been prepared to handle. At least Carlene had planned to participate in this show herself, much to Steve's relief. However, in her haste to be up and about, she'd reinjured one of her legs. And, well, here he was.

"Oh," Kelly-Ann murmured.

Steve stared at her curiously. He was having an awful time sticking to the subject.

"Oh, what?" he asked.

She shrugged. "Just 'oh.' Your oversleeping explains your appearance."

"What's your excuse?" he asked, unconsciously using the question to scrutinize her. Even harried, he couldn't help noticing that the woman had gorgeous dark hair and exceptionally lovely legs.

"My excuse for what?" Kelly-Ann asked.

Inadvertently, Steve stared at her skirt.

"Oh, my skirt!" Kelly-Ann cried. "*I* dressed in plenty of time. I don't want my clothes to get wet," she explained, unusually self-conscious. "I have an eye appointment today."

He nodded. "I have an appointment, too, remember? *Is* Jeffy ready?"

"Jeffy?"

"The dog—the collie." He glanced at his watch. "I wish Suzette was here," he muttered beneath his breath.

He felt at ease with Suzette; she knew he was out of his element with show dogs, that he was doing this for his sister. He didn't mind Suzette seeing him harrassed nearly as much as he did this woman—this Kelly-Ann.

He'd been muttering and mumbling since he rapped on the bell. Still, he wasn't about to go into the whole story of the collie.

Kelly-Ann pressed her lips together in consternation. She wished Suzette was here, too. Her pulse began to race. Jeffy? A collie? There was only one collie in the cages.

George Washington Jefferson IV, also known as Jeffy, hadn't been groomed. The man in front of her was going to be unhappy about that.

In fact, she would bet her half-Irish heritage that he was going to be *very* unhappy. She wanted to be sure what she was up against before she revealed the unfortunate information about the dog.

"Name?"

"George—Washington—Jefferson—IV," he repeated, enunciating each name precisely, as if Kelly-Ann suffered from a hearing loss.

"I need *your* name."

He'd already told her that, too, he thought impatiently.

"Steve Jamison."

"Sign?"

"Sign?" he repeated. "*What* sign?"

"Your astrological sign," she said.

He looked at his watch again. He was going to speak to Suzette about her help. He didn't need this fragmented chitchat, no matter how well-intentioned.

He could recite astrological data. He'd dated enough women caught up in the stars and relationships to be familiar with which signs were supposed to match. He was open-minded; he suspected almost anything was possible in this world.

He also knew that fate could change. This woman's just might if she didn't bring Jeffy out posthaste!

With what he considered commendable civility, he reiterated, "Will you get the dog? I've already explained my situation."

That's not the half of it, fella, Kelly-Ann told herself, trying to buy some time. She had to ask Suzette, who was surely en route to the other shop, about Steve Jamison's dog.

Kelly-Ann needed to stall Steve long enough to let Suzette talk to him. Perhaps she could soften the news since they were apparently on good terms.

Kelly-Ann had no doubt at all this man was going to be uptight when he learned that he had an unkempt show dog. It bothered her terribly. She had an unexpected need to have Steve Jamison like her. She'd felt that the whole room was charged from the moment he entered.

That strange compulsion was overruling her common sense even now! *Why* did she want to know about Steve Jamison?

Ted Haffner had been the man she was thinking of. Ted Haffner, her eye doctor.

Not this man. Not this Steve Jamison, for heaven's sake!

Chapter Two

Kelly-Ann *knew* Steve Jamison didn't want to be delayed, and yet she couldn't stop that damned, determined chattering. It wasn't that she wanted to annoy him, it was just that she had to buy some time.

"You were born in late March, weren't you?" she asked. "The first sign of the zodiac. I'm the fourth one, Cancer, for July." Call it fate, call it curiosity or call it plain stupidity which it no doubt was, she had to know about him!

Steve looked around the shop, then drew in a steadying breath. He didn't know what this woman's problem was. Some of these star-directed personalities were positively neurotic about the day's predictions.

"I was born in February, if it's relevant to your getting my dog," he said. "Not March. February—Pisces. Now will you kindly get Jeffy, or do you need to know his sign, too?"

"You're *Pisces!*" Kelly-Ann cried, shaking her head in amazement. Aries would have accounted for the rash, reckless rush. It would also account for the accelerating temper. But Pisces...

On the other hand, it was true that he'd had the sensitivity to turn red when she'd made a joke about no cardiac arrest in the shop.

"About the dog..." he began again, his voice slightly strained, his mood definitely taking a downward turn. "If I don't see him soon, you might find that I'm running out of patience as well as time."

He didn't want to threaten to get her fired, yet he was fast approaching it. He didn't understand it himself; hurry or no hurry, he wasn't usually this irritable with anyone, but he wanted to be through dealing with this woman.

Uh-oh, Kelly-Ann thought, she needed that typical Piscean sensitivity and understanding for this situation. However, maybe he wasn't a true Pisces. Perhaps he was one of those cusp people who fell under the influence of another planet.

Kelly-Ann truly thought it would be better if Suzette handled this ornery individual. People were fanatic about their ordinary household pets; a show dog was a living treasure. They were literally, in some cases, worth their weight in gold! No doubt Suzette had overbooked with all best intentions; Jeffy had been bypassed in the deluge of last-minute patrons.

Steve stared at the woman. He had a horrible hunch something had happened to Carlene's dog. Although he was doing his best to tamp his temper and squash his suspicions, the woman wasn't helping matters.

Carlene was upset enough by the newest injury delaying her recovery. If something happened to Jeffy... Well, it just couldn't. That was all.

"What are you saying *no* to?" Steve demanded. "Are you saying no you won't get my dog? Is that why you're shaking your head, Miss—Miss—"

"Keernan," Kelly-Ann reminded him, wishing she could give him a groomed Jeffy as easily as she could her name.

Steve managed a smile and tried again. "Thank you, Miss Keernan—it is miss, isn't it?"

He cringed at his own question. He didn't want to encourage more idle conversation with this woman! What was it about her that got him off track so easily?

"Now that I have your attention—again—please allow me to add, the subject is dog. *D-o-g*—Jeffy."

Kelly-Ann unconsciously and nervously traced her full lower lip with her tongue. Steve Jamison wasn't at all indecisive about what he wanted.

What he didn't know was that *she* didn't have the dog groomed!

For a moment, only a moment, Steve was distracted by Kelly-Ann's pink tongue causing her bottom lip to glisten enticingly. Snapping back to attention, he passed the breaking point.

"This is absurd!" he announced, abruptly bridging the gap between them. "I'll get the dog myself!"

He shook his finger at her. "Don't think that will be the end of it! I've tried to be patient with your lectures and your personal philosophy, even after I told you I was in a hurry."

As he moved toward her, his body language left no doubt about his irritation. "Suzette *will* hear about this!"

"Wait!" Kelly-Ann cried. "About your dog. He hasn't been groomed."

"What?" Steve stopped to stare at her.

Her big green eyes gazed at him from behind the round glasses she wore. "I don't know how it happened. I *know* it's upsetting."

"Upsetting!" he repeated. "No! It's inexcusable! That's what it is."

Kelly-Ann nodded. "That, too, if you insist. However, it actually was a lack of communication between me and Suzette—a misunderstanding. I'm really sorry."

"Sorry?" he sputtered. "*Sorry!* Is that all you have to say? I have a dog show and an ungroomed dog, and you say you're sorry?"

She shrugged helplessly, wishing she could do something magical to give this story a happy ending. She *was* sorry, yet there was no way to rectify the situation at this late date.

"I don't know what else *to* say," she murmured contritely, all the light gone from her green eyes.

She could have said that Suzette was beautiful and wonderful with animals, though occasionally not reliable in relaying information. Still, Kelly-Ann would choose love for animals as a trait of her helpers over organization any day.

Except this particular day.

The temper finally reached full fire. "Say you're *kidding!*" Steve Jamison insisted. "Say that you have Jeffy ready!" He held up one hand. "No, don't say anything else. I've wasted enough time. Bring him out here!''

Caught up in the progressing drama of the undone dog, Kelly-Ann hadn't noticed that small, dangerous soapy drops of water had dripped from her hands and vinyl apron as she stood talking. So when she turned, her foot skidded out from under her like an old-time comedy character's.

Before she had time to blush, much less fall, she was supported from behind by wonderfully strong, secure hands. She felt a rush of heat color her face. As crazy as it seemed, she believed the near-accident was inevitable. Steve was *meant* to touch her!

Trying to free herself of the delicious fanciful path her mind was traveling, she managed a breathless, ''Thank you.''

She couldn't deny that, regrettably, she found Steve Jamison very attractive. She knew he would associate her with anger from now on, even if he had kept her from crashing to the floor.

Kelly-Ann had been bitten by dogs and scratched by cats, not to mention other less savory experiences with an assortment of other animals. She'd had a disgruntled customer or two in the past, but she had *never* failed to do the job.

''The dog, please,'' he muttered. ''I don't want anything else to happen before you get the dog.''

His statement brought Kelly-Ann back to reality. ''What kind of work do you do, Mr. Jamison?'' she asked, turning to face him, the evidence of her own temper in the frown etched into her forehead.

''What difference does that make, for crying out loud?'' He shoved his hands in his pants pockets.

"What *is it* with you and all this personal-history stuff?"

"The point is, we all make mistakes," she said, striving for control. "We're sorry. It happens. Even to you, I'm sure."

"When—and if—I make a mistake, it's not of this magnitude," he countered. "This is your line of expertise!"

"And I'm *good* at it!" Kelly-Ann flung the words at him, not one to take an insult. "I know you're angry," she said, "but there's no excuse for being so hateful, for treating me with such—such *contempt*—because of a single mistake!"

Steve was taken aback by the scolding. Ever since he'd come in this shop, he'd been in an uncharacteristic state of confusion. He'd experienced a quickening of his pulse when he touched Kelly-Ann. The heat that had rushed through him had set off alarms. He hadn't the time for anything but retrieving the dog—not the time nor the inclination to get interested in this disorganized dog groomer.

But he certainly didn't feel contempt. If anything, the woman had felt wonderful. She'd smelled wonderful, too. She wore some subtle fragrance that tantalized without overpowering him. He liked that.

"I don't mean to sound harsh," he said, reverting to the reason he was here. "This dog competition today is a chance for Jeffy to give an informal audition that might lead to a part in a commercial." Pleading deep brown eyes met hers. "For the last time, just *get* him."

Kelly-Ann bit down on her lower lip as she moved away, carefully sidestepping the small puddle of water. She wished Steve Jamison hadn't looked at her like that with those beautiful brown eyes. She wished that he hadn't told her how much the competition meant to him.

And she truly wished that she could produce a perfectly groomed Jeffy, if only to see Steve Jamison smile.

Regret in each step, Kelly-Ann trudged to the cage and took the collie out. The sooner she got this over with, the better; yet all the time her mind was racing. Considering all kinds of ways to placate the man, she led the collie into the reception room.

Steve had done his best to be patient. He'd found this woman decidedly inattentive to business, yet disturbingly appealing from the moment he saw her. He had tried to remain civil.

However, the hectic morning proved too much for him. Carlene had wept when she couldn't go to the show and couldn't reach the trainer who had been working with Jeffy on weekends.

When Steve saw the animal at the end of the leash, he went over the edge. Slamming his hand down on the counter, he caused both Kelly-Ann and the collie to jump.

"I don't believe this!" he said in a tight, tense voice.

"Now just a minute," she retorted, her control vanishing. "I told you he wasn't groomed. I won't tolerate that kind—"

"I don't care whether he's groomed or not—"

"What are you talking about? Just what *do* you want?" she asked, wide-eyed.

"I want Jeffy, damn it! That is *not* Jeffy!" Steve practically growled through gritted teeth.

Frightened green eyes protected by soap-splattered glasses met fiery brown ones. Kelly-Ann's heart began to race. *This* was not his dog? Was that what he'd said? No, it couldn't have been.

"Not Jeffy?" she repeated in a tiny little voice she hardly recognized. "This isn't Jeffy?"

He shook his head. *"No!"*

Kelly-Ann tried her best to get the simple fact to register. Saints preserve her, she didn't have another collie in the shop! What had happened to Steve Jamison's Jeffy?

Steve attempted to gain a semblance of sanity as he stared at the bewildered woman. Where was the dog?

In five years of owning her own business, Kelly-Ann had never had this happen. She fled with the collie in tow. Her pulse pounding in her temples, she looked at the dog's name.

"Jimmy," it stated.

Jimmy. Jeffy. Close. The same initial letter. The same number of letters.

But clearly no match.

Oh, God! Why was her mind running aimlessly amok when she had a missing dog? *A missing dog,* for heaven's sake!

She rushed from cage to cage, futilely hoping one of their other animals would turn into a collie before her eyes. She even paused in front of a mixed breed that could resemble a collie if push came to shove. She stared at the name tag, willing it to be the correct one.

Trixie.

It wasn't even a male! Good grief! What had become of Steve Jamison's dog? She couldn't go back out there empty-handed.

She even went to the bathtub and looked at the shepherd-sheepdog mix, knowing that she hadn't left Pierre bathing a collie.

"Psst! Pssst! Kelly-Ann," Pierre hissed when she came close. "Psst!" he persisted in his French accent.

"Not now, Pierre," she said agitatedly, trailing back toward the inevitable confrontation with Steve Jamison. She felt as though she were wearing cement shoes.

She didn't have far to go. Steve was striding toward the swinging door, every hint of restraint gone at this newest delay.

Unfortunately, he wasn't the only one who'd lost patience. The sheepdog, too, had tired of waiting. Suddenly the huge animal scrambled over the side of the wash tub, thudding to the floor, legs splayed, sloshing water everywhere.

Delirious with freedom, his holding leash trailing along behind him, he thundered across the room and darted with amazing agility under the swinging doors.

"Pierre!" Kelly-Ann cried unnecessarily. "Horace is loose!"

"I try to tell you," the Frenchman insisted indignantly. He gestured wildly as he explained. "He pull from my hands and poof! He is gone from the bath!"

Poof, indeed, Kelly-Ann thought wildly. She wished she could go poof and be gone, too!

As though to mock them both, Horace rumbled into the main reception area. His dragging leash caught the bottom of the parakeet's perch and upended it. The small wire door swung open as the cage tumbled to the floor.

As fate would have it, the parakeet made good his escape. The frightened little bird zoomed around like a toy plane guided by a remote control in an excited child's hands, veering this way and that, unsteady and unsure, but determined to fly.

Abruptly, he decided on a course. Right toward the counter. Where Steve Jamison stood staring in renewed disbelief, his face set in taut lines, his posture stiff.

As unhappy coincidence would have it, Horace chose to pursue the panicked bird, who unceremoniously found an unlikely—and dubious—safety zone atop Steve's head.

Steve didn't know what to do. Sensitive to the bird's distress and knowing the woman would need all the help she could get to recapture it, he nevertheless didn't appreciate being a parakeet's perch.

Kelly-Ann reached the rigid customer at the same time Horace did. He, too, seemed uncertain about what to do. Undeterred, he took automatic action as he eyed the parakeet.

Horace began to shake himself fiercely, the soapy water splattering all over Steve's slacks. The dog then lunged up, planting his paws on Steve's chest as he attempted to get as close as possible to the bird.

When Steve automatically reached out to ward off the dog, the parakeet promptly evacuated the premises. Steve seemed to be in shock as he stared at the unfolding drama.

The panicked bird flew wildly, nearly going down a couple of times while Horace happily chased after him, water spraying everywhere as he indulged in what he clearly considered great sport.

Kelly-Ann and Pierre joined the chase, which had by now set off the other dogs again as Horace barked and gave artificial plants and ceramic animals his own brand of bathing as he brushed by them.

The frantic bird was losing air power. He couldn't find a route of escape. He almost crashed into the huge glass window before he did an about-face.

"Duck!" Kelly-Ann cried, hot on the path of both Horace and the parakeet.

It was too late.

Steve Jamison had been targeted.

Kelly-Ann Keernan wanted to sink into the floor and fade away as she watched her unhappy customer duck to avoid the nervous bird.

Chapter Three

Pure survival instinct kept Kelly-Ann moving in the face of dilemma and embarrassment. She and Pierre recaptured the dog and coaxed him to a holding area, then finally lured the bird back into his cage from his resting place on the valance of the window curtain.

Steve Jamison waited, as rigid and red-faced as a painted totem pole.

Frantically reaching for the first handy towel, Kelly-Ann tried to decide what to clean first. To be fair to the man, he stood stoically, statuelike, through Kelly-Ann's ministrations as she wiped at the water on his shirt and slacks.

When she raised herself off her knees, she giggled nervously while she struggled with half-formed apologies and the near lunacy of unleashed laughter.

Steve's beautiful brown eyes were glazed. His voice was low and dangerous, edged with irritation and humiliation.

"Get Suzette on the phone!" he said through clenched teeth.

Kelly-Ann thought he had a great idea. She immediately reached for the phone with shaking hands. She and Steve waited with bated breath as the number at the other shop rang without answer.

Kelly-Ann gnawed on her lower lip when she had to hang up. Suzette hadn't reached the shop yet. Kelly-Ann was being forced into the position of telling Steve that they didn't have his dog.

Just as she replaced the receiver in the cradle, the phone suddenly rang, causing her to jump two feet into the air.

Deliberately avoiding the harassed, dogless, splattered Steve Jamison, she picked up the phone and held on for dear life. After all, it was a line to somewhere, a link to something stable.

"Hello," she said in a scratchy, breathless voice. She cleared her parched throat. "Hello. K.K.'s Perfection Pets, er—Petfections—K.K's P-p—"

She exhaled a breath that caused loose strands of hair to blow. Mortified, not daring to look at Steve, she licked her lips and tried to say something sensible.

"If you're calling the dog grooming shop, please hold."

"Dog Grooming Shop?" the party on the other end said. "No, that's not the shop I want." Annoyed, the caller hung up with an abrupt bang.

Deserter! Kelly-Ann thought. Then, suddenly an idea that seemed heaven sent occurred to her. Maybe, just maybe Steve hadn't booked Jeffy in this shop. Maybe he'd made a mistake.

She didn't allow herself to think about the fact that he knew Suzette. After all, someone *else* could have taken the dog to the wrong place. *Anything* was possible.

Anything *had* to be possible. She *didn't* have his dog!

Without looking at Steve, she licked her lips and tried again. "If you're calling the dog grooming shop, you got it. Please hold."

Cowardly, never acknowledging that the other person had hung up, she used the excuse of the phone call to scour the pages of her appointment book. She prayed every second that Steve Jamison had left his precious pet elsewhere. For her sake, his, Jeffy's and Suzette's.

Her prayers went unanswered.

She almost uttered something unseemly when she saw Suzette's scrawled notation of George Washington Jefferson IV's arrival.

Where could Jeffy be? There was a strict store policy that an animal was never transferred from shop to shop in order to avoid upsetting both animal and owner.

Kelly-Ann was suddenly overcome by an anxiety attack. Jeffy was missing! Maybe kidnapped, or an escapee! Her thoughts raced on, each worse than the last until she was left with no recourse but to face Steve Jamison.

Attempting to build courage, she turned back to the phone as though she were answering a question for the party on the line. The phone rang again, and Kelly-Ann glared at it. Some help it was!

"Busy day," she muttered.

"Suzette!" Steve reminded her, the one pointed word coming at her like a dagger. "I want to speak with Suzette."

The phone stopped ringing, then started up again. Chickenhearted, Kelly-Ann postponed the awful announcement about Jeffy for another moment.

"Hello. K.K.'s Pet Perfections. Please hold," she said with deliberate speed, determined not to stumble over the name this time.

When Kelly-Ann correctly announced the shop, it finally occurred to Steve that he might be dealing with the owner. Surely the initials K.K. and the name Kelly-Ann Keernan weren't coincidence. He knew better than to assume anything, but he had thought Suzette owned the shops because she gave the difficult job of bathing large dogs to Kelly-Ann.

And because, he reminded himself, Suzette had left that impression when he dealt with her. If Kelly-Ann was the proprietor, the wrong he'd been done seemed even worse. It was one thing for an employee to make a mistake of this magnitude, but for the shop owner...

Abruptly, he strode past Kelly-Ann into the animal-holding area, intending to find his dog and get the hell out of here.

"Mr. Jamison, you can't—" Kelly-Ann cried anxiously.

"Kelly-Ann!" the voice on the phone yelled so loudly that Kelly-Ann put the phone back to her ear.

"Suzette, thank God!" she cried. "Do you have Jamison's collie?"

Tensely, she awaited the reply. Before she heard it, the irate owner of the missing dog returned and spun her around to face him.

"Where is my dog?" he demanded, his hands firm on her shoulders.

Pierre appeared from out of nowhere. "What are you doing, you idiot man? You leave Kelly-Ann alone!" he ordered, striking Steve's hands with balled fists.

That was the final indignity, the proverbial straw that broke the camel's back. Taking all of his anger and frustration out on the smaller man, Steve freed Kelly-Ann to grasp Pierre by the shirt collar with one hand.

"Stop that! Stop that this minute!" Kelly-Ann demanded, tugging on Steve's arm. "Oh, you nasty man! If you'll only listen, I have Suzette on the phone! You're going to get your dog!"

At least she hoped he was, she thought, her pulse racing again.

For a moment, Steve appeared stunned by his own behavior; he felt incredibly foolish, as though he should ask if the smaller man was all right. Their eyes met as Steve released a red-faced Pierre.

Embarrassed, Steve reached for the phone as if it were a lifeline. "Suzette, where's Jeffy?" he asked in a hoarse voice.

Her hands clasped in a prayerful pose, Kelly-Ann leaned closer in an attempt to catch some of Suzette's conversation. She couldn't hear a word, but she watched as Steve's eyes remained stormy.

"I *do* understand how that could have happened with the boss you have," he said. "Miss Keernan is your boss, isn't she? This is her shop—and that one, too, no doubt.''

Kelly-Ann wished she could hear Suzette's response, but it was impossible. She glanced over at a furious Pierre, who stood glaring at Steve. She understood how the Frenchman felt.

Steve Jamison couldn't leave soon enough to please her. She didn't care if he never brought his dog back! Who did he think he was to grab Pierre like that? She thanked her lucky stars that Suzette had Jeffy and had groomed him.

Steve looked at Kelly-Ann. Brooding brown eyes encountered frosty green. She had a feeling that this man rarely lost his cool, but the morning's progressing fiasco had been his Waterloo, indeed! His dark gaze held hers briefly before he glanced at the gold watch on his wrist.

"I'll talk to you when I get there, Suzette," he said into the mouthpiece, effectively ending whatever explanation Suzette was giving him. "I don't need to tell you that I'm already later than I expected to be, and I was running late when I arrived! Still, I *may* be able to make the show, after all.''

He replaced the receiver and headed for the door without addressing Kelly-Ann again. The phone rang before the door could close behind him.

"K.K.'s Number Two Pet Perfections," Kelly-Ann answered with forced cheerfulness. She wanted to collapse in relief now that the awful man had left her shop.

Suddenly she was reminded of the hateful man who lived in her own neighborhood. He had actually called her up and told her she was a bad neighbor because she had so many animals at her house. He hadn't given her a chance to explain that they had nowhere else to go.

She detested bullies! Even worse, she despised people who had no sympathy, no concern for other inhabitants of the world around them. People like Steve Jamison and the meanie who lived across the fence from her.

"Whew!" she said aloud. And her horoscope had predicted *positive* interactions today! She didn't want to find out what the negative ones were.

Unfortunately, she was about to.

"Oh, Kelly-Ann!" Suzette wailed from the other end of the line, "this is dreadful! Steve is one of my newest and best customers. Why, I wouldn't have had this happen for the world. What are we going to do?"

"First we're going to calm down," Kelly-Ann said with more conviction than she was feeling. "This is a mistake. He's the one who's overreacting. Boy," she said more to herself than to Suzette, "he's sure not a typical Pisces."

"You met him on a bad day under circumstances that would cause anybody not to be at his best," Suzette insisted. "Honest, he's something special, and I hate to lose him."

Kelly-Ann suppressed the thought of how attracted she'd been to Steve. She would not allow herself to recall the memory of his hands on her skin, but she couldn't deny that the room seemed chilled and empty now that the dynamic man was gone. If only there had been some way to stop the escalating craziness....

Nonsense! she told herself. She and Pierre had done nothing but defend themselves. The chill she felt was only the aftermath of a very bad scene.

She *preferred* to dislike Steve Jamison. *February man. Pisces!* A personality so confused that his symbol was two fish at odds with each other!

How appropriate for him, she decided. At least he was a true Pisces in some ways. Despite wanting to soothe Suzette, she couldn't regret the loss of Steve's business.

"I'm sorry, Suzette. I don't share your opinion of that man. I can't begin to tell you how he behaved when I couldn't produce Jeffy. I was a wreck! I didn't know what to do after I couldn't find the animal. In fact," she almost whispered, "I brought out Jimmy by mistake."

"You didn't!" Suzette moaned. "Don't you see that Steve has a right to be upset? He's in a hurry. He couldn't get the dog. Oh, dear me, Steve's *still* in a hurry," she murmured, dispiritedly, as though it had just registered on her.

"Well, why on earth did you take Jeffy over there anyway? That's exactly why we have a rule about—"

"I know, I know!" Suzette interrupted. "I was up to my elbows in dogs when Steve came whirling into shop Number Two where you are."

Kelly-Ann couldn't wipe away the sudden, vital image of the man in her mind. She knew what Steve looked like when he was whirling: his hair disorderly, his tie undone, his— Oh, this was absurd!

She didn't care what Steve Jamison looked like as long as she never saw him again herself!

"After I booked Jeffy and Steve rushed off," Suzette continued, "I remembered that today is the day we switch shops. I would be over here. I needed to bathe

Jeffy and he would be over there. I tried my best to bathe him last night, but I ran out of time. I knew I'd have to come in early to do him, so I tried to phone you to tell you I needed to transfer him to shop Number One. You didn't answer.''

"I was there at the shop,'' Kelly-Ann said. "I didn't get home until seven-thirty.''

"I tried the shop twice. No one picked up,'' Suzette said.

Kelly-Ann nodded. She'd heard the phone ring, but she was in the middle of bathing a dog and couldn't answer. In truth, she hadn't thought much about it.

"I worked late, too,'' Suzette interjected. "After I couldn't reach you, I tried Steve so I could tell him how behind I was. No one answered. I decided I would take Jeffy to this shop and get up early to groom him. I had every intention of calling you and Steve to let you know.''

"You didn't reach either of us,'' Kelly-Ann murmured, disappointment and accusation mingling in her voice.

"No!'' Suzette cried, as distressed as the other woman. "When I got home, I was so exhausted I fell asleep in my bathtub. I knew I had to go to bed or I wouldn't make it through today's workload. I didn't even think about trying to call again.''

Her voice rose even higher. "Kelly-Ann, you know I can't get out of bed. I slept right through my seven o'clock alarm!''

"Well, it's said and done now,'' Kelly-Ann mused. She *did* know that Suzette was a night person. The bottom line was that she'd done her very best.

"Don't fret about it anymore," Kelly-Ann added consolingly. "At least you *have* Jeffy and you groomed him. You can't imagine—"

"No," the usually boisterous Suzette said in a meek voice.

"No, *what?*" Kelly-Ann gasped. "You *do* have the animal, don't you?"

"Yes," Suzette murmured. "I have him, but I *didn't* groom him. I forgot all about him."

"You didn't!" Kelly-Ann cried, her chagrin renewed. "Please say you didn't! Tell me Steve Jamison's dog has been groomed."

Good grief, she was beginning to sound like Steve Jamison himself. Impatient. Unsympathetic. Contemptuous of Suzette because of a mistake. *Of course* the woman hadn't groomed Jeffy. She'd just arrived at the shop!

Suzette sighed forlornly. "For whatever reason—I didn't remember Jeffy until I saw him in the cage. Then it was too late! Oh, glory, Kelly-Ann, Steve will be so upset. He thinks Jeffy will be ready for competition. This is important to him because of Carlene."

Kelly-Ann didn't know who Carlene was, but it didn't matter at the moment. What mattered was what they both *did* know: Steve Jamison would be *so upset!*

In fact, he would probably be downright *hostile* this time.

"Say something!" Suzette cried. "I didn't do it on purpose!"

Kelly-Ann tried to decide what to say. The dog's not being groomed was bad, it was true.

All right, it was *terrible!* But in view of the situation, at least they had the dog. He hadn't disappeared completely as Kelly-Ann had feared.

"What will I tell him?" Suzette moaned. "Kelly-Ann, *talk* to me!"

"Tell him the truth, and if he gives you any trouble, call me and I'll talk to him," Kelly-Ann said, thinking how much easier it was to say that when Steve Jamison was headed to the other shop.

"Oh, glory, he's here!" Suzette exclaimed. "Don't hang up, Kelly-Ann. Stay on the line for moral support. I'll put you on the speakerphone so he won't know."

"Suzette," the other woman murmured, "it was an honest mistake. Don't you dare let that man badger you."

"You don't understand. He'll be so disappointed."

Suzette's voice faded, and Kelly-Ann heard the click as the woman switched to the speakerphone and replaced the handset.

"Steve, I'm sorry about the mix-up," Suzette said animatedly, camouflaging the panicked reaction of seconds ago.

Kelly-Ann smiled to herself. No man could resist Suzette. Everything was going to be okay. But just in case, she crossed her fingers for good luck.

Tense, she listened while Suzette empathized with the man for having to go all the way across town.

For a moment, Kelly-Ann didn't hear Steve speak at all. She couldn't know that he was studying the shop.

Steve had never been to shop Number One. He was immediately reminded of Kelly-Ann Keernan. Warm

and homey, with a personal touch that shop Number
Two definitely didn't have, the room was a reflection
of Kelly-Ann as she'd been when she first talked to
him: sunny, vibrant, a bit out of the mainstream, yet
comfortable and soothing.

There were two rocking chairs with homemade
cushions—and real live cats in them, right there in the
reception room!

He groaned. He didn't want to stand here and com-
pare that woman to the atmosphere in this shop. It
bothered him that he'd known Suzette for several
months and really liked her, yet now she and shop
Number Two seemed deliberately focused, as though
business was what mattered. Of course, that's the way
it *should* be. He realized that.

And it wasn't that Suzette wasn't a beauty and a
dream to work with, but she seemed—he didn't want
to think it—indiscriminatingly patronizing. He refused to use the word *insincere,* because he didn't believe it. Still, she didn't have the compassion and
concern that Kelly-Ann had.

Nor did she waste time with idle chitchat and talk of
horoscopes and sun signs, he reminded himself firmly.

"That boss of yours," Kelly-Ann heard Steve murmur. Then to her frustration, he spoke so low she
couldn't understand the rest of his words. Her fingers
tightened around the receiver. She told herself she
didn't care what he said, though, of course she did.

She didn't need to strain to understand what happened next. Suzette announced that Jeffy hadn't been
groomed.

"What?" Steve demanded. "Not groomed? I don't believe this! Not after the time I just spent in the other shop! Why didn't you tell me?"

"I tried," Suzette insisted. "You hung up."

Unexpectedly, the man's voice was filled with disappointment, as Suzette had predicted.

"Talk about bad luck," he said unhappily, "the show today is such a rare chance. Jeffy could be the biggie of his dog generation. Or, rather, could have been," he lamented. "He'd be good in commercials. He has charisma, charm, personality. Carlene—"

"I know, I know," Suzette commiserated. "He's clever, he's beautiful and he's definitely not a little automaton like many show dogs."

Don't push it, Kelly-Ann thought as Suzette poured on the empathy, yet Kelly-Ann felt awful about Jeffy's missed chance at stardom. Steve did sound disappointed.

And Suzette was right. He had a reason to be angry.

Then Kelly-Ann realized he wasn't angry—just disconsolate, now that he'd located his pet and was dealing with Suzette.

Saints above, that somehow made it all worse! Now *Kelly-Ann* wanted to console him!

"I'm *so* sorry, Steve," she heard Suzette saying. "What if I bathe him real fast, or at least trim him a little?"

"It's too late," Steve said. "This is my fault, too. I shouldn't have raced into the shop with him last night, but the show was rescheduled quickly because of the talent scout and snow. Everybody in dog-show circles had to hurry."

"Yes," Suzette said, then added something Kelly-Ann couldn't hear.

"No," Steve said all too plainly. "Brush him as best you can to make him as presentable as possible. I've got to go. A scroungy dog is better than none. I'm afraid we'll have to make do this time."

Kelly-Ann couldn't contain herself. She and Suzette were in the wrong; she wanted to try to help make it right. After all, the shop had promised Steve a groomed dog, and they were not delivering.

"Steve," she burst out before she thought, "maybe this has all happened for the best. I know you probably don't think much of horoscopes, but I do read for dogs, and maybe this just isn't going to be Jeffy's day."

"What the devil?" Steve muttered, staring at the woman in front of him.

At the end of the line in the other shop, Kelly-Ann was busy fumbling beneath the counter, looking for her astrological charts. "If you can just tell me when he was born—"

"Suzette, did you know the speakerphone was on?" Steve asked. "Did you know that woman was listening to our conversation?"

Kelly-Ann didn't hear Suzette say anything; she could imagine the woman shaking her pretty head.

His voice indicating Suzette had betrayed him, Steve ordered, "Get my dog, please."

As Suzette hurriedly complied, Kelly-Ann quickly pulled the animal's history from her files. Jeffy's birthday was recorded, as well as other relevant facts. She rapidly set about making a prediction for the day for him.

Kelly-Ann was filled with optimism. Jeffy was going to have a wonderful day for travel and money! Surely that meant he was going to win.

"Steve? Steve? Mr. Jamison? I've finished, and you're going to be pleased about this!" she said enthusiastically.

Suzette came on the line. "Kelly-Ann, he's gone. He just walked out of the shop with Jeffy."

Chapter Four

Kelly-Ann wavered for only a second. "Go get Steve Jamison, Suzette, and bring him back. Tell him I have something important to relay."

"Please do *something* to put him in a better mood," Suzette implored.

"I hope to," Kelly-Ann vowed.

"Hello," came the curt, irritated voice across the wire after a brief pause.

"Mr. Jamison, this is Kelly-Ann. Listen, I want to encourage you to go on to the dog show. Jeffy's going to do fine. His chart shows—"

Once again she was holding on to a dead phone. Steve Jamison had hung up!

Kelly-Ann picked up the newspaper that was lying on the countertop and slammed it down. Boy, he was a thankless man! She didn't know why she was bothering! She stabbed the push-button numbers for the other shop and clasped the receiver tightly to her ear when Suzette answered.

"Kelly-Ann, he hung up."

"I know that," the indignant brunette said. "Go after him again, Suzette, and bring him back!"

"Kelly-Ann—"

"*Now,* please! I don't care what you say to lure him. I want him at the other end of this line!"

While she waited, her blood pressure rising, she stared down at the paper. The horoscope section was before her.

After a few more seconds, Steve came on. He honestly didn't know why he was such a glutton for punishment. He had the dog. Why had he let Suzette drag him back?

"What *is it?* he demanded. "Haven't you delayed me enough?"

"No, not quite!" Kelly-Ann snapped. "You, Mr. Jamison, are the rudest, most self-centered man I've ever encountered. Don't ever, ever bring your dog back into my shop! In fact, don't step foot anywhere near me, you—you wishy-washy, feeble-brained fish!"

Wishy-washy, feeble-brained fish! Steve thought. Just who did that dimpled darling think she was? Did she *really* think he would bring Jeffy back?

"Don't worry, you *chattering, criticizing crab!*" he countered. "I have no intention of doing so."

Crab he'd called her! Kelly-Ann thought incredulously. Boy, he was a fine one for using that word!

"By the way," she noted crisply, "*your* horoscope says romance is in the stars for you today, believe it or not. I suggest that you grab any *other* caring person who comes your way. I'm sure you need all the love you can get. And, another thing, take off your pants—''

"What?" he exclaimed. "Take off my *pants?*"

"Yes. Not only are they water splattered, they don't match your suit coat. Jeffy may not be groomed, but I'm sure he looks neater than you do. Instead of worrying so much about him, try to make yourself presentable. Comb your hair, too. Your cowlick is showing!''

Steve was stunned by her second scolding of the morning. He paused, searching for the right response. He wasn't about to admit to any of the complimentary adjectives that surfaced. She was a good-looking woman with gorgeous green eyes, lush hair, full figure and lovely legs.

It was her mouth that was her downfall. He could visualize Kelly-Ann as clearly as if she were standing in front of him, her cupid's-bow mouth outlined in pink lipstick. That beautiful cupid's-bow mouth that caused the most delightful dimples to appear in her rosy cheeks when she smiled.

A grin slowly crept across Steve's mouth as he stared down at his pants. He *was* color-blind; although he could tell one color from another, he couldn't distinguish shades.

In truth, it irritated him to know he didn't have control over something as simple as color choices. A few of his friends periodically matched his clothes for him, but he'd had to wing it since Carlene's accident, asking her about shades only if she was awake when he left the condo.

His own carefully structured social life had dribbled down to nearly nothing with his younger sister an unhappy invalid in his house.

This morning Carlene had been so disappointed about not being able to go to the show that she'd slept late. Steve would no more have awakened her than he would have prodded a hibernating bear!

And he *did* have a cowlick! He'd detested it since he was a boy. It was another of the things he had no control over, no matter how he combed it or had the barber shear it.

"Is that all?" he almost purred into the phone after a lengthy pause.

"Definitely!" Kelly-Ann shot back, then slammed the receiver down.

Steve gently replaced the phone on his end. Gently and thoughtfully.

Kelly-Ann stared at the receiver. Well, now Steve Jamison knew what a crab really was!

She pursed her lips as she contemplated the exchange. Sure, she'd called him a wishy-washy, feeble-brained fish. He had vacillated several times; that made him wishy-washy in her opinion. Feeble-brained, she didn't know about. Maybe that had been unfair.

And she was a crab, of course—if he was speaking of the symbol for Cancer.

She suddenly smiled. That sly devil *did* know something about the zodiac!

As quickly as she'd smiled, she frowned. Clearly Steve had meant to insult her; he'd unintentionally managed to get her sign right.

She waited a minute, then pushed the redial button for the shop.

"It's Kelly-Ann," Steve told Suzette when he heard the phone ring. Then he once more got Jeffy in hand, albeit somewhat leisurely, considering he'd rushed around like a mad dog all morning. "She is a crab, you know," he added casually. "That's her sun sign." Then he chuckled and left the shop.

Out on the street he was consumed with thoughts of Kelly-Ann Keernan, this woman who by sheer chance had happened into his life with her bright chatter, inquisitive nature and nuttiness! She was something else! She was vital, she was outspoken, and she was persistent.

He liked confidence in a woman. Now that he took time to think about her, he'd liked many of her personality traits, too many, not to mention the good looks. And that temper! When she let that loose, she wasn't playing.

But she was right: he had been rude. He'd deserved her temper. In fact, he'd savored it! He was glad to realize she was passionate as well as nurturing.

The door had closed behind Steve when a thoroughly confused Suzette answered the phone.

"He did call me a crab, didn't he?" Kelly-Ann asked.

"Yes," Suzette murmured. "He knows you're a Cancer."

"He does?"

"Yes. And you know what else, Kelly-Ann?" Suzette said, her voice high.

"What?"

"He chuckled when he left."

"He did?" Kelly-Ann murmured, a bit dumfounded by the revelation.

Now she was as confused as Suzette, but wondering about it would simply drive Kelly-Ann completely crazy!

She was concentrating on it so much that she didn't even tell Suzette goodbye or hear Pierre come up behind her as she replaced the phone.

"What did that savage say?" Pierre asked. "I should have beat him with these two hands," he declared angrily.

Kelly-Ann blinked. The last thing she wanted was to have a hair on Steve Jamison's handsome head harmed, despite her annoyance with him.

Anyway, Steve could have beaten the stuffing out of poor Pierre, though she wouldn't hurt Pierre's feelings by saying so. She reminded herself that he'd attempted to come to *her* rescue.

"He didn't say much," she answered evasively. "Suzette hadn't groomed his dog. She forgot. Steve wasn't as mad as he might have been."

"If he returns to this shop again, I will beat him to a bloody—bloody pain," Pierre improvised.

"You'll do no such thing!" Kelly-Ann shot back before she thought, "and anyway, you mean *pulp*," she supplied automatically, her mind preoccupied with Steve Jamison.

She'd helped Pierre with his English since his arrival at her shop. He was a skilled groomer, marvelous with animals—and *patrons*—now that she thought about it.

Of course, Steve Jamison had completely missed Pierre's charm. But then, she didn't think anyone could have charmed that man!

"I promise you," Pierre insisted, "if that man comes before me again, I *will* beat him. I, Pierre, will defend my honor. I didn't do it the first time because you came in my way, but next time—''

"Pierre, there will be no next time!" Kelly-Ann insisted.

A brooding look crossed Pierre's darkly handsome features. "I don't comprehend," he muttered. "Why are you…" He gestured with one hand while he sought the right word. "Why do you give support to this man?"

"For heaven's sake," Kelly-Ann murmured, "you know the customer is always right. And, unfortunately, in this case, this one really was."

"He was *not* right!" Pierre declared. "He has no right to—to storm trooper the back. No customer is right to do that."

"Pierre," Kelly-Ann said soothingly, "we've worked together two years. Some people are difficult. Steve Jamison was one. Now, please, let's just put this behind us and get on with the day."

"No," Pierre insisted stubbornly. "I must take a footing on this. If the man comes back, I tell you there must be a battle."

"Pierre, Pierre," Kelly-Ann said with a sigh. "Please don't make an issue of this. Not today of all days."

She knew how mercurial Pierre could be, ranging between high and low moods, sensitive at one moment, explosive at another. He, too, was a Pisces, she recalled.

Right along with his compassion came the coolness, the need to periodically retreat into a cocoon and become unapproachable.

His moodiness was the one thing that kept him from being the perfect employee, even though he rarely erupted in a fit of anger. She had that uneasy feeling that today was going to be the day. She tried once more to ease the discord.

"We've both been under a strain," she noted. "Poor Horace is still wet. Let's finish his bath and get back on schedule so I can keep my eye-doctor appointment."

"*You* wash Horace!" Pierre snapped, suddenly removing his apron. "I quite."

"*Quit,*" she corrected impatiently, then wondered if she'd lost her mind. She didn't know why she was correcting Pierre's English at such a crucial time. She didn't want to lose Pierre!

"And you can't *quit!*" she cried. "We have too many clients."

"I, Pierre, am a man," he declared. "Do not think you, a woman, can tell me my—*affairs!* My honor has been dirtied today, and I *will* quit! The customer is always right! Baa!" he fumed as he stalked away.

"Wait, Pierre!" she cried.

"*Adieu!*" he called over his shoulder.

Kelly-Ann flinched as he slammed the door behind him. Good grief, what a knack she had with men! First Steve Jamison, then Pierre! She supposed she would manage to upset and anger Ted Haffner, her dream eye doctor, before the day was over.

Oh, dear heavens! She wasn't capable of coping with more catastrophes! Her energy had been geared toward positive interactions today!

She honestly didn't understand what had happened with Pierre. She'd never anticipated him walking out.

She exhaled wearily, blowing long strands of hair from her face.

When would she ever learn how to deal with the opposite sex? How was she ever going to find the husband she wanted when she seemed to have so little understanding of the colossal male ego? Her biological time clock was running. She wanted babies! Lots of babies!

And that required a man—a husband. Unexpectedly, a larger-than-life vision of Steve Jamison loomed in her mind. He was on a white horse, his curly hair in disarray, his clothing flying in the wind....

Steve stroked his chin as he watched the progression of the dog show. He didn't know what he was doing here, much less *how* to do it. He had little hope of accomplishing anything, but he'd had to come for Carlene's sake.

He hadn't accomplished anything. He was no professional. He hadn't felt competent to show the dog without a handler or his sister giving advice. He'd done what he could and hoped Jeffy would win something, anything, to boost Carlene's spirits.

He hadn't even known in which category to enter Jeffy. He'd explained his plight to one of the judges and considered himself lucky to be allowed to show Jeffy at all. It hadn't done any good; Jeffy hadn't even placed. Steve knew Carlene was going to be disappointed, but the dog's chances had been extreme at best.

Steve had little belief that the talent scout, wherever he was, would notice Jeffy, either; still, he would stay a bit longer just in case a miracle happened. He felt bad about going home and telling Carlene he'd failed, regardless of how ridiculous the odds were against Jeffy.

Besides, he couldn't make any more of a fool of himself than he already had this morning. After that scene in the dog shop earlier, he didn't intend to lose his temper again. Kelly-Ann Keernan had managed to make him recall how enraged—and inadequate—he'd felt when he'd learned his fiancée was after his money instead of him.

He couldn't explain why the dog-shop owner made him remember things he wanted to forget, things he'd thought he'd dealt with a long time ago. Apparently he hadn't quite gotten the bitter taste of bad love out of his mouth.

Oh, he'd regained his self-confidence easily enough, now that he thought about it. He might not be Kelly-Ann's idea of a prince on a white horse, but he hadn't had any trouble finding enough women to take the dents out of his ego. Thankfully, they'd healed his heart and his masculinity.

He'd even let up on long work days—mainly because Carlene needed him. If any good could be found in her accident, it was the new direction both of their lives were taking.

Carlene's confinement had necessitated that Steve and she take time out of their busy lives while she mended. Carlene had become so engrossed in dogs that she'd decided to change her proposed major in college to something animal related.

Steve had been forced to slow down and think while he stayed at home with his younger sister, helping break up her boring days. Like lightning, it dawned on him why Kelly-Ann Keernan had the power to bother him, to agitate and disturb him!

He hadn't thought of marriage a single time since his fiancée left her bitter legacy. Not a single time, no matter how many beauties bounced into his arms, until he encountered Kelly-Ann with her lushness and warmth, her green eyes and extraordinary legs, her dimpled cheeks and sweet voice.

All of a sudden, Steve was in a hurry to leave. He wasn't serving any purpose here anyway. He stood up abruptly, Jeffy's leash in hand and turned toward the door. Instantly, he bumped into a large buxom woman, almost toppling both of them.

"Pardon me," he said, bracing her with some effort. "My fault."

"Yes, it was," she said curtly, then she moved to one side.

Unfortunately, Steve moved in the same direction. The two of them engaged in a waltz with clumsy steps for a few seconds, darting and dodging, bumping and butting, stepping on each other.

Shaking his head, Steve muttered, "I really am sorry." He wanted to tell her if she'd just stand still, one of them could get by.

Jerking Jeffy's leash, he stepped back so the woman would have a clear path. Jeffy, responding to the command Steve didn't know he'd given, slumped down on the floor, right in the woman's path.

She toppled over the dog, landing on the floor, her skirt up, her slip showing, one heel twisted under her shoe.

"Oh, my God, I am so sorry," Steve said.

What a day! What an awful, awful day for dealing with women. He reached down to pull her up, and the task was almost his undoing.

Fuming, breathing hard, she struggled to her feet somewhat ludicrously in the broken shoe.

"I can't tell you how sorry I am," Steve repeated. "Are you all right?"

When she glared at him, then at Jeffy, Steve decided he'd done enough apologizing. And had enough accidents today. He wanted to go home where he was safe and secure and free from frantic and fierce women.

Except Carlene. Carlene, who was going to be so disappointed. But that couldn't be helped. As fast as his feet would carry him, he headed toward the door, Jeffy at his side.

"Young man! I say, young man! Come back here!"

The raucous, commanding voice halted him in mid stride. What did that battle-ax want now?

He exhaled as he retraced his steps. "Come on, Jeffy," he grumbled. "Let's get this over with." When they reached the woman, he asked, "Is there something else?"

"*Only,*" she said imperiously, lifting arched red eyebrows, "if the collie is yours. Otherwise, there is *nothing* else, I assure you!"

"I see," Steve murmured, half to himself and half to her.

He didn't know what it was about today; he couldn't seem to get along with women. Usually he didn't have that problem.

Or did he? Damned if he could remember at the moment. He'd already promised himself he wouldn't lose his temper after upsetting both Kelly-Ann and Suzette.

Oh, yes, and there was Pierre. When he'd been face-to-face with the other man, he'd seen fear and shame in those dark eyes.

A new rush of regret overtook him. He wasn't a rude, impatient bully, and he was embarrassed to have anyone think of him that way. He'd acted badly because of the woman Kelly-Ann. He knew it was no excuse, but she'd had him so turned around he'd forgotten why he'd gone to the shop. There was just something about her—

"*Is* it your dog or *isn't* it?" the voice boomed near his ear.

Steve shook his head. The woman looked as if she might take off her broken shoe and strike him if he didn't answer.

"It *isn't!*" she stated, obviously in response to him shaking his head. "Then, pray tell, do you have the capacity to inform me whose dog it *is?*"

"I didn't say it wasn't mine," Steve noted, thinking that this scene, too, had already taken place in a similar vein at Kelly-Ann's grooming shop. "I—"

The steamroller didn't give him a chance to finish!

"Not *another* one!" the burly redhead said, rolling blue eyes highlighted with black mascara. "What is *wrong* with you people here at this show?" she asked, hinting at a disastrous morning herself. "Do you know anything about your animals?" she continued, that voice grating on Steve's nerves. "Or is it *yourselves* you don't know about?" She patted an incongruously fluffy upswept hairdo.

Steve couldn't help noticing the diamonds she wore on her hand as she moaned, "Why *does* Elroy send me to all these places? Jordan got to go to Africa to check out zebras."

She turned on Steve again before he could offer any sympathy, which he'd tentatively begun to suspect she might need. "All I've asked for is a simple yes or no, but you Southerners are *sooo* slow! *Is* that your dog, or isn't it?"

Steve stiffened, all empathetic thoughts evaporating in the face of her rudeness. He'd had a bad day, too. Who did this battle-ax think she was? What difference did it make to her if Jeffy was his dog or not?

Abruptly he recalled trying to get an answer from Kelly-Ann about Jeffy's whereabouts. It had been a frustrating experience, to say the least. However, he'd had some right to ask about the dog.

Then it suddenly occurred to him that perhaps this person had some reason to question him about dog ownership.

"Yes," he said. "It is my dog."

"Then why did you shake your head no?" she demanded irritably, rolling those blue eyes again.

Steve stared at her. She reminded him of his worst nightmare! What was it about these women today, battering him with inane questions? Still, some intuition warned him to keep a civil tongue.

"The dog is actually my sister's. Why do you ask?"

"Why?" the woman repeated, as if he were a moron. *"Why?"*

"Yes, damn it! Why?" Steve was losing control.

She looked at him sternly, then her hard features relaxed a bit. "It's been a *dreadful* morning for me." She sighed dramatically. "My plane was late coming in from California, no one met me at the airport, my rental car is a joke, and I had to rush right here to the show." She glanced down at her shoe. "And now *this.*"

Clearly she wasn't finished. Glaring at the plane ticket still jutting out of her sweater pocket, she announced, "This is my *fifth* trip in *eight* days. I've been running all over the country looking at dogs! Little dogs, big dogs, short dogs, tall dogs, furry dogs, hairless dogs. I want to get this over with!"

Gesturing with a long-nailed hand, she pointed to the show floor. "Nothing. All these dogs and *nothing* that might work."

She looked back at Steve. "Except for her. Young man, *I'm* Nina Bromberg, the talent scout all of you have been panting for, and I may just have someone who's interested in casting her in a commercial."

The talent scout they'd all been panting for, indeed! Steve thought. He didn't give a hoot in hell who she was.

Well, maybe a small shout, he had to admit. Now wasn't the time to air his temper—again. After all, this was why he'd come.

Carlene would be ecstatic at Jeffy actually being considered for the commercial. It sounded too good to be true.

Steve fought for control. "Do you have some identification?"

With a flourish, the woman produced a bold black-and-white business card that appeared to have her condensed history on it. It also had her name and picture. Convinced she was the scout, excitement stirred in Steve for his sister's sake.

"Sit down," Nina ordered, motioning with the be-ringed hand to two nearby chairs on the sidelines.

Steve barely had time to lead Jeffy forward before the woman literally plunked him down in one of the chairs, a ham of a hand on his shoulder.

"I'm worn out from all this," Nina said, waving a dismissing hand at the dogs that were still being shown.

It wasn't until Nina sat down and pulled off her shoes that a small unwanted word registered in Steve's mind. Nina had referred to Jeffy as "she." Maybe the scout was looking for a female. If that was the case, Carlene's dreams would be dashed.

Steve watched as the woman took out a pair of thick-lensed rhinestone glasses and put them on. No wonder she hadn't found a dog she liked! She probably couldn't see without her glasses!

And she thought Jeffy was *female*. Steve wished she hadn't even singled him out. When the dog slumped down disconsolately on all four legs and began to whine, Steve reached down and stroked the animal's head.

"It's all right, boy," he murmured gently. "We'll leave in a few minutes." He was sure this wouldn't take long.

He had a sudden vision of Kelly-Ann chasing Horace around the reception room; Kelly-Ann with her sweet voice and love of animals. She'd been wonderful with the dog and the parakeet. He smiled. She hadn't been too bad with him, either. That is, until she laughed.

Suddenly Steve laughed aloud. It had been damned funny! He just hadn't been in the mood to appreciate it at the time. Wouldn't it be something, he asked himself, if Kelly-Ann was correct in her horoscope reading for Jeffy, as improbable as it seemed even at this stage of the game?

He grinned and shook his head. If—and it was a big if—since Nina appeared to want a female dog for this commercial—if Kelly-Ann was right, surely it was coincidence.

He didn't know what to think. Only one thing was sure for him at the moment: he'd been thinking of Kelly-Ann Keernan nonstop since he met her!

Chapter Five

Kelly-Ann squirmed in the ophthalmologist's chair in Ted's office. She didn't know what was wrong with her today. She kept going over and over her confrontation with Steve Jamison.

Now that she was here, Ted Haffner didn't seem nearly as important as he had when she'd planned this visit. He was very attentive, more so than usual, but she didn't feel like romance now.

She looked a mess! She'd had to bathe Horace by herself, as well as two other dogs, and she hadn't had time to even pin her hair back up. Ted was as much a stickler for punctuality as—as Steve Jamison, and she hadn't wanted to be late for her appointment.

Then *she'd* been kept waiting! She didn't know why she'd rushed about madly. What was so great about Ted Haffner, anyway? she asked herself, following his instructions as he tested her eyes.

For some reason she seemed to be seeing him in a different light. Odd, but she didn't care if she won him over or not. She didn't know what had changed since she'd made the appointment.

"Kelly-Ann!"

"What?" she snapped, coming abruptly out of her reverie.

Ted chuckled. "Testy today, aren't we? Well, that's fine, as long as we remember we're in the doctor's chair having our eyes examined. I asked you to read the line most clear to you."

Kelly-Ann felt her face redden for what surely must be the fifth time. "I'm sorry, Ted," she muttered. "It really has been one of those days."

He studied her for a moment in the darkened room, causing her to wonder what he was thinking. She hadn't had time or the energy to do anything about her appearance after she'd wrestled Horace back to his cage by herself.

"All you need is a little attention," Ted said, his voice more soothing than she'd ever heard it. "I'll take you out to dinner tonight. Some wine and pasta, and you'll be as good a new."

"I can't go, Ted," she said, finding it ironic that she'd intended to entice him today, and now that he was asking her out, she had to refuse. "I'm much too busy at the shop. I have to work late. Pierre quit," she said with a sigh. "I'll never get finished."

"Pierre quit?" Ted repeated, clearly surprised. "Why?"

Kelly-Ann really didn't want to go into it, but she'd started; she had to offer some explanation. "He lost his temper when I told him the customer was always right.

This particular customer *was* right, though he was also nasty."

"About what?"

She didn't want to go into it, yet she was too tired to think of anything except the truth. And she didn't want to go into *that*.

"It's a long story," she said evasively. "We didn't have his show dog ready. He rushed into the holding area—" She frowned. "In fact, we didn't even have his dog—I mean, we did have it, but at the other shop. Oh!" she cried, "I don't want to discuss it now. Ted, I'm in a terrible hurry, and . . ."

Her words trailed off lamely. Oh, God! She was sounding more and more like Steve Jamison!

"I'm sorry you had to wait. I had an emergency," Ted told her. "You know how those things happen, Kelly-Ann."

"Yes, yes," she agreed impatiently, then felt ashamed of herself.

"I'm sorry, Ted. You know how people are about their animals, too. I'm so far behind that patrons will be furious when they find out they can't pick up their pets today."

Unexpectedly, Ted scooted his mobile chair next to her stationary one and cupped her face in his hands. "Poor baby," he murmured, "you're in serious need of some tender, loving care. And *I* mean to be the one to provide it. I understand perfectly how harassed you are and that's why I insist that we go out tonight."

"I can't!" she declared, tugging his hands away from her face.

It was hard for her to believe that hours ago she had been eagerly anticipating this time with Ted. Why did things have to look up between them right now, when she couldn't handle an impossible day, much less romance?

"I really want to see you," he whispered persuasively, reaching out to take one of her hands in his.

"I can't see you tonight!" she all but exploded, pulling her hand free. Great Scot! Didn't the man understand English?

She sighed wearily as she tightened her hands into fists and listened to her thoughts echo inside her head.

Of course, Ted Haffner understood English. The kind of English she'd been praying to hear; the kind she'd asked the stars to help her initiate; the kind she'd hoped her horoscope for today implied.

Now, she *didn't* want to hear it. She wasn't a fickle woman by any stretch of the imagination. What had happened? Surely it was just the events of the morning.

She leaned back in the chair and closed her eyes. Surely it was the *event* of the morning: Steve Jamison.

Steve tried to keep his eyes and mind on the road as he returned from Greensboro, North Carolina to Martinsville, Virginia. It was difficult. Very difficult.

Jeffy hadn't won the dog competition, but he'd earned an audition for the commercial. In Hollywood, California!

Kelly-Ann Keernan's predictions had been right, for whatever reasons. Everything *had* worked for the best. Ironically, Jeffy had been selected solely because of his less-than-perfect grooming.

The talent scout, Nina Bromberg, hadn't cared whether he was male or female. She'd said ordinary

American households could relate to Jeffy. The trend was to make everything more believable in commercials, including the actors.

Jeffy just might be the next big "ad" dog. Maybe, Nina had said, the next big "movie star" dog! Steve looked over at the animal sitting in the front seat of the sports car.

He was sure this was more than enough to lift Carlene out of the doldrums and get them both into a more satisfactory routine. This was the incentive, the *miracle*, Carlene needed to get well and allow both of them to get on with their lives.

"Good boy, Jeffy! You did it!" he praised lavishly.

Although Jeffy clearly didn't know what he'd done, he appeared pleased anyway. He panted and wagged his tail happily, seeming to grin as he looked at Steve. Then he gave the man a big lick across the face with his long, rough tongue.

"Enough, enough," Steve said, pushing him away. He found the gesture above and beyond the call of duty. "Listen, boy, I'm not fond of your kisses," he noted. "I prefer mine from a woman with red lips."

A picture of Kelly-Ann Keernan flashed into his mind. What *was it* about that woman that intrigued him so? He made himself turn his attention back to Jeffy.

"Settle down before I buckle you up. We've got to get home safely. You're going to be a star, and Carlene is going to be ecstatic! We've finally done something right today!"

He frowned. He certainly couldn't take credit for the way things turned out. After all, if Suzette hadn't forgotten to groom Jeffy, this particular commercial possibility might not have come about. Steve considered himself especially lucky since the morning had begun as an unmitigated disaster.

But the person he wanted to talk to was not Suzette; he wanted to talk to Kelly-Ann. He definitely owed her an apology. He didn't know why he'd overreacted this morning.

He pressed his lips together. Yes, he told himself, he'd already determined earlier that he *did* know: it was the woman herself! He wished he could say that Kelly-Ann Keernan had struck a wrong chord in him with her endless delays, her lectures and lack of attention to business.

But that wasn't all. Why, he'd probably been in the shop less than five minutes. *He* had behaved badly.

He did know he'd been out of line and owed it to her to say so. Anyway, he wanted to tell her that her predictions had come true. At least the one for Jeffy apparently had.

Steve was eager for Kelly-Ann to know how the dog show went. More eager than he could understand. And definitely more eager than he should be!

Kelly-Ann sat in a chair at Ted's office, her eyes closed while she waited for them to adjust enough for her to put on dark glasses to drive back to the shop. The office visit had been a fiasco! She couldn't believe it!

She'd come in looking like a witch who'd fallen off her broomstick, her hair a mess, her skirt with folds and wrinkles where it had gotten wet while it was pinned up, and she had dog hair all over her blouse.

Then Ted had turned the tables for the first time and tried to get the romance between them rolling. It was what she'd been hoping for, praying for.

Or so she'd thought, before Steve Jamison came into the shop and caused such an upheaval.

Darn Pierre! When he'd walked out, he'd left her in a real bind. She'd finished Horace's bath, all right, but she'd ruined what was left of her attempts to look good for Ted. Not that Ted had seemed to notice, much to her annoyance.

The *real* topper was that she hadn't been able to concentrate on Ted while she was in the chair with him only inches away. She hadn't been able to look into his eyes and see the reflection of the children she wanted mirrored there. She hadn't seen anything at all.

Except an image of Steve Jamison!

Steve parked the car in K.K.'s Number Two Pet Perfections' lot and got out. With a leashed Jeffy in hand, he went up to the shop and tried to open the door.

Geez! After he'd hurried all the way here, the place was locked up. A homemade sign said Kelly-Ann would be back around two o'clock.

He looked at his watch. It was after that now. Where was she? He'd picked up a newspaper himself and read his own horoscope for the day. Then he'd read Kelly-Ann's. He was absurdly anxious to see her!

"What am I going to do?" Kelly-Ann asked Suzette as the two women worked on a toy poodle, attaching pink ribbons to each ear while the little animal waited patiently to be made pretty.

"How could you let Pierre quit?" Suzette asked.

"I couldn't stop him!" Kelly-Ann exclaimed. "You know Pierre! Good grief!" she muttered. "What a day! What a *nightmare!* We've got to find someone else! I'm so far behind."

"And *I'm* so far behind," Suzette said. "At least you have a helper. Now Pierre won't be coming over to help me in the afternoons."

"Oh, no!" Kelly-Ann exclaimed. "I forgot about Lisa. I must get back to the shop. There's no one to let her in, and it's almost time for her to get out of school. Heaven knows, I need her today."

"I'm responsible for this trouble," Suzette said miserably. "Let me call Pierre and talk to him."

"He needs to cool off a bit," Kelly-Ann said wisely. "Then we'll see if we can get him back." She ran a hand through her hair. "Saints preserve me, I look a mess."

Suzette responded with unconscious honesty. "You do. Did you see Ted looking like that?"

Kelly-Ann evaded the question as she smoothed down her hair again. Suzette hadn't needed to be so quick to agree!

"That's a story for another time. I've got to run by the house. I need to see to my animals before I meet Lisa at the shop. Talk to you later."

As she hurried out the door, she thought how Steve had rushed into her shop hours before. It had been a day full of upheavals and misunderstandings, all starting with Steve. . . .

Steve walked into the pet shop where Suzette was busy trying to bathe a feisty cocker spaniel who was shaking water everywhere while he howled as if he were being mistreated.

The dog groomer didn't see Steve approach, and he wasn't about to touch the bell on the counter. He'd been cured of that in the other shop.

When he went to the tub, Suzette jumped.

"I'm sorry," he said. "I can't seem to do anything right today. I didn't mean to startle you."

Suzette tried to smile. "Steve, *I'm* the one who should apologize. Everything that's gone wrong is because I forgot Jeffy."

"No! That's why I'm here," he said cheerfully. "It was a splendid day for me because you *didn't* bathe Jeffy. Please don't apologize. I'm the one who acted badly. I'm the one who's sorry."

Suzette was taken aback. It had been a strange, unsettling day. Clearly, she didn't understand what Steve was talking about. Before she could comment, he continued. "Kelly-Ann's not at the other shop. I'm trying to find her."

"You are?" Suzette asked suspiciously.

Steve nodded. "Where is she?"

"She's on her way back to the shop," Suzette said, still baffled. "She went to her eye doctor's office during lunch hour and she had to wait."

"That's right," he recalled. "She said she had an appointment."

Suzette sighed wearily. "Apparently it went as badly as her morning." Then she looked as if she'd let the cat out of the bag, her blue eyes wide. Kelly-Ann despised for Suzette to discuss her personal affairs.

"What do you mean?" Steve asked. "Did she get some bad news about her eyes?"

"No, no," Suzette hastened to assure him. "It seems things didn't go as she'd planned with Ted."

"Ted?"

"Ted Haffner, her ophthalmologist."

Steve was dying to ask what Kelly-Ann had planned with Ted, yet he wasn't sure he wanted to know. Although it was too early to speculate about how extensive his own interest in the woman was, he did want to get to know her.

What if she had a serious relationship with this Ted Haffner? Was there more than a doctor-patient relationship? He'd have to find out for himself.

"Thanks!" he called, already turning away.

"Steve!" Suzette called after him. "I—ah—I don't really think Kelly-Ann wants to see you!"

Steve grinned. "Sure she does," he said confidently. "She just doesn't know it yet."

Kelly-Ann arrived at the shop just as Lisa did. She almost crashed into the girl when she rounded the corner from the parking lot.

"Hi," she greeted the lanky teenager. "I'm afraid I've got bad news for you today, Lisa."

"You're not going to fire me, are you?" the girl asked nervously, a worried expression altering her face as she tugged at braided hair.

Kelly-Ann almost choked. What had happened to the *positive* interactions forecast for her today? "Good heavens, no!" she quickly assured the girl. "Pierre quit! I need you more than ever."

"I'm sure glad to hear that!" Lisa was clearly relieved. "Not that Pierre quit," she clarified, "but that you need me. You rattled my cage there for a minute. I'm saving money for college.''

"Good.'' Kelly-Ann was decidedly relieved herself. To use Lisa's expression, Kelly-Ann's own cage had been rattled almost past repair. "I was going to ask if you could work tomorrow.''

Lisa shook her head vigorously. "Uh-uh, I can't do that. Saturday is the only day I can spend with my boyfriend.''

So much for worry about the job, dedication to work and saving money for college, Kelly-Ann thought. Still, she'd vowed she wouldn't lose her patience again today.

A part-time worker was better than none, even if the shop owner was in a jam and had hoped Lisa would help. Love was love, Kelly-Ann supposed, and a boyfriend might be more important to a young girl than work.

Maybe to a woman, too, she told herself, wondering what she was going to do about Ted and why all her plans had gone awry.

At that moment, Steve walked up and clasped her hand as though she were a long-lost friend, making her gasp in surprise.

What did *he* want? She hadn't thought she would see him again—except in her mind, where he'd been naggingly persistent.

"I'm glad I caught up with you!'' he said warmly, causing her suspicions to soar. "I've been looking everywhere.''

Kelly-Ann was confused; maybe *she* didn't understand English. Was *this* the man who'd hung up on her and vice-versa this morning? She didn't understand why he was so exuberant.

"Have you had lunch?" he asked.

"No." She hadn't had time in all the confusion.

"Great. I'm starving. Let's go eat. I want to tell you about the show."

The show. The dog show? Why was he looking so pleased? "Did Jeffy win in any category?" she asked hopefully, buoyed by Steve's high spirits.

"Nope."

The man *grinned* as he said it!

Thoroughly befuddled, Kelly-Ann stared at him. She didn't know about him, but she didn't want any more bad news!

She snapped back to reality and pulled her hand free.

"I'd love to hear what you have to say, Steve, but I can't listen now. I've had an awful day, and we're terribly behind." She turned to the girl. "This is my part-time helper, Lisa."

She unlocked the shop door, opened it and started in. She couldn't endure a repeat of the morning. She didn't understand why this man was so congenial when he'd said Jeffy didn't win! Was he setting her up, getting ready to really tell her off?

Steve grasped Kelly-Ann's hand again and drew her back toward him. "Lisa is perfectly capable of overseeing the shop for a short time, aren't you?" he asked the girl.

Lisa lit up like a hundred-watt bulb. "Yeah, I can do it alone," she bragged.

Kelly-Ann realized Lisa hadn't even glanced at her since Steve walked up. The teenager looked as though she'd been struck by lightning—Steve Jamison lightning.

"Steve, I can't go," Kelly-Ann insisted, wondering why the words sounded so familiar. Hadn't she said them to Ted about dinner? "Everything's so chaotic."

"Yes," he agreed. "You look like you're riding a lightning bolt." He repeated the words she'd said to him this morning. "You need to calm down. I won't allow you to have cardiac arrest. Unless it's over me," he added teasingly, his smile irresistible.

That was a definite possibility, Kelly-Ann thought as she brushed at her loose hair. He didn't look like an angry man. He didn't appear to be mad. He sounded quite pleasant.

And the warmth of his hand around hers penetrated all the way to her thudding heart. She was acutely aware that she did want to hear what he had to say.

At least she thought she did.

Good grief! She was becoming as indecisive as a Pisces! And all because of this man!

Chapter Six

"Steve, why are you smiling if Jeffy didn't win?" Kelly-Ann demanded. "Why are you being nice to me? Why are you holding my hand...? I declare, Steve Jamison, why don't you make a decision and stick to it? You said you were never coming back to this shop!"

"I have made a decision," he said defensively.

He had *never* thought of himself as indecisive. Quite the contrary, he'd always considered himself as very much in control, very much decision oriented, living a structured, planned life.

But maybe that wasn't true these days. Ever since Carlene and Jeffy—well, now wasn't the time to debate with himself about it.

"I came back with the explicit intention of being nice to you," he announced. "I owe you an apology, but there's more I want to say."

Kelly-Ann sucked in her breath. *He did? There was?*

And damn! Oh, why did this man have such an effect on her? Why hadn't Ted's touch been as provocative as Steve's?

"Come on," he coaxed, his voice almost unbearably sexy. "Have lunch with me. That is," he said, looking down at his clothes, "unless you're ashamed to be seen with me. I really couldn't blame you."

"Ashamed?" she parroted. How could any woman be ashamed of this handsome man?

He indicated his hair, a tiny smile dancing at the corners of his mouth. "I still haven't had time to do anything about this cowlick or these mismatched clothes."

Kelly-Ann tried not to stare at the playful smile on his devastatingly appealing lips. Wanting to look anywhere but at this man who set off such a potent reaction in her, she gazed at her own clothing. Suzette's frank assessment came to mind.

She'd forgotten how mussed she herself was. She gave Steve a woeful glance. She hadn't minded Ted seeing her this way nearly as much as she did Steve. No wonder he'd made that comment about her riding a lightning bolt!

"Look at me!" she cried. "I can't go to lunch like this."

For a moment Steve was so distracted that he forgot why he was here. Kelly-Ann's voice was not only sweet, but had a breathless, sexy quality to it when she was distressed.

"You look beautiful," he whispered, taking her—and himself—by surprise with the seriousness of his compliment. She *was* in a state of disarray, but it hardly mattered at the moment. He wanted to be with her so much, he couldn't think of anything else.

Kelly-Ann self-consciously brushed at her dark hair.

Unable to resist, Steve reached out and let his fingers run all the way down the length of the wavy strands that had fallen forward over her shoulder.

He wasn't lying. Kelly-Ann did look beautiful to him.

Of course, he hadn't been able to get beyond her hair so far. He had thought it was lush and lovely atop her head, but loose down her back and around her shoulders, it was even more luxuriant than he had imagined. It framed her face perfectly, setting off those dazzling green eyes behind her glasses.

Kelly-Ann knew she was a wretched sight, but how could she resist such words? Could this be the same man who'd dashed into her shop and thrown a tantrum this morning? This February man. This—

When she heard Lisa sigh, Kelly-Ann remembered they were standing on the sidewalk with the shop door open and her teenage helper gawking at Steve.

The girl didn't seem much in the mood for work now, and neither did Kelly-Ann. Saints above! *She* was gawking at Steve, too! What was it about this unstable, moody Piscean that managed to stir her up in ways that no other man had in months?

"You do need to calm down," Steve reiterated, shoving his hand into his pocket as if it had been terribly errant.

"I do?" Kelly-Ann murmured, coming out of her stupor.

Good grief! Was his effect on her that apparent? Did he hear her hammering heart or feel the heat from her hand? Could he see in her face how pleased she was by his compliment?

"You said so yourself," he reminded her, even though he was using her phrase from this morning when he told her she needed to calm down. "You've had an awful day. You'll start the afternoon in a better mood if you take a break."

Kelly-Ann was grateful that she wasn't a walking neon sign proclaiming Infatuated With Steve Jamison. And heaven knew she *did* need to calm down—from the effects of him!

Maybe he was right: a break might help her work better after the turmoil of the morning. But *with* him?

Kelly-Ann looked at Lisa. The girl *was* capable of tending the shop—if she could function after staring at Steve for so long. Kelly-Ann looked back at Steve. *Yes!* she wanted to cry. *Yes,* to lunch, *yes* to today, *yes* to tomorrow.

Discreetly inhaling a steadying breath, she managed to sound amazingly nonchalant. "All right," she agreed. "But for no more than an hour."

"Fine," Steve said. Then he winked at Lisa as he squeezed Kelly-Ann's hand.

"By the way," he said, "can we leave Jeffy here?"

"Jeffy?" she murmured. Did anything else in the world exist except Steve Jamison?

"Yes, he's been in the car a long time."

"Oh, yes! Yes, of course," Kelly-Ann exclaimed. How stupid of her. Jeffy, the dog! Jeffy, the reason she was with Steve. The missing Jeffy of just a few short hours ago.

"Why don't I get Lisa to groom him?" she offered.

"That's not necessary," Steve said. "You have enough work to do, as you've already pointed out."

Although she knew she should insist upon the grooming, she also knew he was right about her being behind. She watched Steve as he went to the car to get the dog.

What did he want to talk to her about? She was ridiculously eager to know! Her mind started to race, and she was glad when he led her to the car. At least she could look out the window and pretend she wasn't totally immersed in the man beside her.

Or so she had thought. When they settled into the car, Steve produced a bunch of buttercups from the back seat. "For you," he said simply.

Steve watched her reaction. Giving flowers to a woman wasn't a thing he would have done ordinarily. He wasn't a man who liked to buy on impulse, and when he did get flowers, he purchased roses. Yet they hadn't seemed right for Kelly-Ann. The buttercups reminded him of her: sunny and bright and warm.

She held them near her heart, absurdly touched by the gesture. "Thank you, Steve. How sweet of you."

"It's the least I could do after this morning," he said, meeting her eyes.

Kelly-Ann was so surprised that she couldn't think of anything to say. There it was, that sensitivity she had wanted to see in Steve. Her silly heart began to soar!

In minutes, Steve had driven to a restaurant up on a hill. Kelly-Ann knew the place well. Ironically, it was the same Italian restaurant Ted had wanted to take her to tonight.

She shook her head. Funny how things had gotten twisted around so quickly. It just showed how fast fate could change! Here she was with Steve after turning Ted down when her intentions had been to entice Ted into a more passionate relationship!

And even worse, this was where she wanted to be. With this mercurial, unpredictable Pisces! This handsome man who whirled into her shop and stormed out. This Steve Jamison who showed up unexpectedly with flowers! With *buttercups* of all things! He couldn't possibly have known they were her favorite, could he?

She didn't know what to think. She was still sitting in stunned silence when Steve came around to her side of the car and ushered her out, taking her hand once again.

Every time he did that, a flush warmed Kelly-Ann's entire body. She didn't know what on earth she'd do if the man ever actually took her in his arms! She'd probably have heat stroke and expire right on the spot!

"Is this all right?" Steve asked.

"What?" Kelly-Ann gazed at him intently, trying to decide what he was asking her. Was *what* all right? Him holding her hand? Despite her heated reactions to his touch, she didn't want him to let go.

"The restaurant." He smiled at her, and her foolish heart skipped a beat.

"It's fine. I've been here often."

"With some of your many boyfriends?" he teased aloud, secretly thinking that now was an opening to find out about Ted Whoever—the ophthalmologist.

"No," she said. "Not exactly."

She didn't have many boyfriends. Only Ted, the Scorpio she'd believed she wanted to marry. And maybe she still did, she assured herself. After all, Steve Jamison was just a customer who'd caught them all up in an unexpected escapade where one thing had led to another.

"Not exactly?" Steve persisted. "Does that mean you don't have many boyfriends or you're not seriously involved with a particular one?"

He didn't want the cards stacked against him with this woman should he decide he was really interested. He wanted to laugh at his own thoughts. Really interested, indeed! He was interested, all right.

Kelly-Ann considered the question. Regardless of what created her interest in Steve—the situation, physical magnetism, electrical currents or plain old hormones—it was enough to let her know that she wasn't as ready for marriage to Ted as she'd thought.

"I'm not about to walk down the aisle," she said, trying to make a joke. She'd sure thought she was when the day began!

"Good! Let's celebrate! We'll start with wine," Steve said, guiding her to a small table at the back of the restaurant. "I know an excellent vintage they serve here."

"Fine," she said, then wondered why all of a sudden everything was fine. And what on earth were they celebrating? She didn't have time to linger over lunch. She was without her primary helper and although she'd left Lisa in the shop alone before, it had been only for a brief time.

Besides, people were going to start coming in to pick up their pets; she'd have more Steve Jamisons on her hands. She had to get back and call some owners to tell them their animals wouldn't be ready until tomorrow. And at that, she didn't know how she'd manage. She'd be at the shop until midnight at this rate.

After they had been served a glass of white wine, Steve held his up. "To Kelly-Ann," he said softly, "who doesn't want to walk down the aisle." He felt absurdly relieved that she wasn't involved with her eye doctor, and he did see it as cause for celebration. To his surprise, a frown creased Kelly-Ann's features.

Boy, she thought, he was sure happy she'd said she didn't want to walk down the aisle. She shifted in her chair as she lifted her glass, then set it down.

In all honesty, she couldn't drink to his toast. He'd misunderstood her. Or rather, she confessed to herself, she'd inadvertently misled him—again.

"Steve, listen, it's not that I don't want to be a bride," she said, glancing away from the merry twinkle in his eyes.

Good grief! She'd never seen a man so happy to think he'd found a woman who didn't want to get married. She realized that she was crushed to discover that.

Steve stared at her. Had she lied? *Was* she involved with the eye doctor? This woman was impossible!

"Then you do want to," he murmured, incredibly let down by the news.

Kelly-Ann was uncharacteristically temperamental. "Of course, I want to!" she exclaimed, feeling tears at the back of her eyes. It was just that she didn't know if she ever *would* be! Certainly not if she kept tripping over men like this one.

"What woman doesn't?" she demanded defensively. "I want lots and lots of babies!" she burst out, feeling like an idiot, unable to stop all the words that seemed to be dammed up at the back of her tongue.

She'd felt that way since the first time she looked at Steve Jamison. She wanted to talk and talk, to explain about herself and her hopes and her dreams. She wanted to hear about his. And all *he* wanted to do was gloat over a misunderstanding!

A misunderstanding that made them a blatant mismatch!

Steve looked puzzled, then chagrined. "Babies by the eye doctor?"

Kelly-Ann shook her head, completely frustrated. "No, not by the eye doctor!"

Well, that was plain enough, she thought, the admission confirming her worst suspicions. So Ted was out of the picture and she was left with no daddy for her babies. Clearly not this Pisces, who'd been *elated* to erroneously think she didn't want to get married.

Kelly-Ann tried to gather her wits about her. Sitting across from Steve with the width of the table—and their diverse desires—between them, she could think better. She got right to the point of lunch, because clearly there was no reason to make any other point.

"What do you want to talk to me about?" She glanced at her watch. "Time is racing. I've been off schedule all day."

Steve stared at her. He thought they *were* talking. She didn't want to marry the eye doctor. But she had said she wanted lots of babies.

"How many babies?" he asked. As soon as the question popped out of his mouth, he felt foolish.

Kelly-Ann pressed her lips into a firm line. She wasn't discussing her dreams with *him!* How many babies she wanted clearly wasn't any of his business.

"Time was the last topic," she said tersely. "I'm in a hurry, and you, of all people, know about hurries."

"Yes," Steve said, easily reaching across the table to take *both* her hands in his. She was driving him crazy, running hot and cold.

"You've already told me you're in a hurry, Kelly-Ann, remember? Do you also remember that we're taking an hour for a relaxing break before you go back to work? Only this morning, you told me what a shame it was to rush about."

Kelly-Ann wasn't sure she remembered anything. Steve holding one hand had been exciting enough. Now she felt as if both her hands were burning. Or was that just a reaction to his touch as he intertwined their fingers?

She wanted to pull free, but he was looking at her with those intense brown eyes, mesmerizing her until she was speechless and spineless. She didn't believe she could draw away if somebody yelled *fire!*

"First, I want you to accept my apology for this morning," Steve said. "I was rude. I was self-centered. I *was* a wishy-washy, feeble-brained fish!"

Oh, how Kelly-Ann wished she wasn't putty in this Pisces's hands. He'd already told her all she needed to know: the incredibly disappointing fact that he didn't want a woman who wanted marriage.

Despite knowing that, Kelly-Ann couldn't hold back a giggle. She must have taken leave of her senses when she called this man names.

"I'm sorry, Steve. I got carried away. You are a fish—being a Pisces, and I believe you have been a bit wishy-washy about some decisions, but I went too far when I said feeble-brained."

Steve chuckled. "Oh, I don't know. I believe that may have been in order this morning. Though I think you'll find that I'm fairly bright. Anyway," he said in a more serious vein, "I'm the one who needs to apologize. You were right about everything. Will you forgive me?"

Kelly-Ann was trying to find her voice when Steve freed her fingers and began to stroke one of her hands. "What's this?" he murmured, his face showing concern as he met her eyes again. "What happened?"

She rolled her eyes heavenward in a silent plea for strength to resist Steve Jamison. He was dangerous. She attempted to focus on her hand.

"It's just a scratch," she said somewhat breathlessly. He was using his index finger to delicately trace the tiny red line on the inside of her wrist.

She hadn't even been aware that she'd been injured, but she was acutely aware that Steve's tantalizing touch on her delicate skin sent shivers up and down her spine. Why, the way he touched her was positively—positively intoxicating! That's what it was!

Steve drew her wrist to his mouth and gently kissed the small scratch, his lips moist and warm and full. "There," he murmured, taking her hand in both his and cupping it. "A kiss is supposed to make a wound heal faster. Did you know that?"

Was he kissing—er—kidding? she asked herself. All that kiss had done was send her blood pressure zooming. She may have used a little peroxide on the scratch if she'd noticed it, but now she doubted if she'd wash her wrist before she absolutely had to!

"Are you going to forgive my bad behavior?" Steve asked, causing her to stare at him in befuddlement.

What bad behavior? Surely not the kiss! It had been exquisite. So romantic. So like the sensitive Pisces men she'd always heard about.

"Kelly-Ann, you really must be exhausted," he commented. "You're not even talking to me, and I need to know if you'll forgive me for this morning."

"Oh, that," she said, hearing the hated faint huskiness in her voice, which was as sure a sign of discomfort as a blush.

She heard other strange sounds inside herself. Was that loud, rapid thudding her heart pounding? Or was it the rush of her pulse like a river racing in her veins?

Would she forgive Steve? Surely this charming, eloquent, deliciously sensual, good-looking man hadn't deliberately done anything wrong. And if he had, she wanted to be the first one to forgive him. For *any-thing*. For *everything*.

"It's okay," she managed to say, speaking as if she had a reasonable degree of intelligence, when she was sure all her brain cells had gone on the blink the moment when Steve's lips touched her wrist. "I told you, it was all a misunderstanding," she said. "We should have had Jeffy ready."

"If you had, he wouldn't have won the audition for the commercial!" Steve explained. "It was because he looked so ordinary that he was selected. Nina, the talent scout, said the public wants animals and people they can identify with these days. If Jeffy had been groomed to the nines, he wouldn't be going to California."

Kelly-Ann tried to digest it all. Jeffy was going to audition for a commercial. In California. Where Steve was going. No doubt with Nina, the talent scout.

Her excitement paled suddenly. She plummeted to earth once more as if she'd been ejected from a rocket that had missed its target. How could she plunge so far down after such an ecstatic high seconds ago?

Steve Jamison's Piscean traits were rubbing off on her. Now she was getting gloomy. She should have been happy about his news, yet all she could think of was that he was going away to California with Jeffy.

And, no doubt, Nina.

She should be happy about that, too, Kelly-Ann reminded herself firmly. Steve and she were certainly no match. Surely she wasn't stupid enough to entertain any more ideas of such a ridiculous union. She'd already ridden the roller coaster of her emotions more times than she wanted to think about.

And she'd only known the man a single day! Nothing like this had ever happened to her. No man like Steve had ever happened to her. She was all out of sorts again!

"Congratulations on the possible commercial," she eventually had the good manners to murmur. Talk about rude. She couldn't seem to think of anything but herself!

"Thank you," Steve said, still holding her hand warmly in his, the stroking movements increasing. "*Everything* you said came true. It was amazing."

Kelly-Ann finally had enough wherewithal to draw her hand back and lock her fingers together in her lap. Why was she enduring the tantalizing torture of his stimulating touch?

"Everything?" she repeated.

Did that mean that Steve had found romance today? She had to know, even though she was well aware it was none of her business. After all, she'd advised him to accept any caring person he encountered.

"What's Nina like?" she blurted.

Steve frowned. "Nina?"

What a strange question in view of all he'd told her! He'd expected her to show some real interest in Jeffy's potential as an actor. After all, she was Jeffy's dog groomer.

His frown deepened. Well, *she* wasn't actually the groomer; Suzette was. But Kelly-Ann owned the shop, he reasoned.

He looked down at his hands, aware that the warmth of her small hand was gone. He hadn't even thought to tell Suzette about the commercial audition. He'd wanted to tell Kelly-Ann.

Kelly-Ann couldn't avoid noticing Steve's frown. There he went again: elated one moment, annoyed the next. Then, of course, Nina wasn't any of her business. She didn't care for people prying into her private life. But surely a romance hadn't developed between Steve and the scout this quickly.

Or had it? She was questioning everything now. That wasn't like her. As absurd as it was, she had to know about this Nina person.

"Nina," Kelly-Ann said. "Didn't you say that's the talent scout's name?"

Steve nodded, not seeing the relevance but willing to engage the question. Maybe Kelly-Ann knew other people who had aspirations for their dogs, or maybe she herself had.

"She's something else," he said with a half laugh, thinking of the battle-axe woman. "She had nothing but good things to say about Jeffy. She thinks he'll be

a commercial hit. I can't wait to get home and tell
Carlene," he announced. "She'll be—what is it she
says—'terrifically thrilled'! This is possibly the best
thing that could have happened."

He pulled Nina's card from his pocket, but now
Kelly-Ann didn't have the slightest interest in the scout.
Who was Carlene? Steve couldn't wait to go *home* and
tell Carlene?

Good grief! Had she been fantasizing about a married man? Daydreaming about babies when he probably already had children? She felt faint. This was
worse than she'd imagined!

Much worse!

Chapter Seven

When Steve handed Kelly-Ann Nina Bromberg's card, she took it with a trembling hand. The talent scout's picture was on it. The fact that Kelly-Ann imagined Steve wouldn't be personally interested in the woman did nothing to calm her. *Carlene* had become the pressing problem.

"Nina invited me to lunch," Steve said, "but I couldn't wait to get back home."

Kelly-Ann interrupted him. "And I can't wait to get back to the shop," she said.

Nina was none of her business; Carlene was none of her business.

"Congratulations again!" She tried to muster some enthusiasm. "I really have to go, Steve. I'm sorry. I shouldn't have come."

"Nonsense," he said, clasping her hands again. "We haven't ordered lunch. I'm not through talking. Your horoscope says positive interactions today. Maybe it means me," he said, his eyes sparkling, his manner eager, as though he was really interested in her.

Kelly-Ann exhaled. She hadn't realized she'd been holding her breath. "My horoscope? What do you know about me?"

He pulled a folded, torn piece of paper from his coat pocket. "I bought this."

"Why?" she demanded. She didn't trust this man one whit, him with his wild mood swings that kept her guessing constantly. She couldn't figure him out. He was as bad as Pierre. What *did* he want from her?

It suddenly occurred to her that his interest could be because she was a dog groomer and could be useful to him. But she wasn't even Jeffy's groomer. Besides, the talent scout had supposedly been sold on Jeffy's natural look.

"I wanted to see what your horoscope said since you'd told me mine," he explained. "Romance is in the air for me, and positive interactions for you. Don't you find that interesting?"

Was he serious? Or just teasing her?

"You didn't seem too interested in the zodiac when I talked with you this morning," she noted dryly, trying to ignore the implications of his last statement. Why *had* he looked up her horoscope?

"That's not exactly true. I'm interested. I just didn't have time to discuss such things then," he said jovially. "Now I do."

Kelly-Ann glared at him, recalling all that had gone on because of Steve and his hurry this morning. Good for him. Everything had gone well for *him*. *He* was on cloud nine. *His* Jeffy was maybe about to strike it rich.

And now he had time for Kelly-Ann—for whatever reasons.

"Pardon me," she said testily, "but don't you think Carlene might object to you having a—a—" She was at a loss for words. "A romantic interest?"

He looked puzzled for just a moment. "Carlene? Of course not!"

Kelly-Ann stared at him. "No? Well, just who is *Carlene-at-home* who won't object to your romantic involvement?"

Steve shook his head. This woman constantly amazed him with her questions and changing moods. Abruptly, he recalled that he'd seen no reason to go into the Jeffy–Carlene story this morning.

"Carlene's my sixteen-year-old sister, Jeffy's owner," he said, launching into a lengthy explanation.

As he spoke, Kelly-Ann realized her heart had started that crazy beating again. His sister! Her dog! An injured leg! She did recall Suzette mentioning a Carlene! It just hadn't mattered to her at the time.

Oh, God! She was feeling topsy-turvy and wanting to flee. This man drained her so! She couldn't get a grip on her emotions. She needed time and distance from him.

She stood up abruptly, dizzy with all that had gone on inside her in one day. "I really must get back to the shop." Her sanctuary, she thought frantically.

Steve was more confused than ever. What was with this woman? She was jumping around as if she was on a hot rock.

"Don't go," he urged. "Where's Pierre? He can surely handle things, even if Lisa can't. Please, sit

down and talk. I'll be frank with you. That split personality of yours is driving me nuts, and I'm doing my
best to focus here.''

Her split personality! she thought incredulously.
Was he joking? What about *his?* Good grief, they'd
been together one day and were driving each other
mad!

She sat back down without pondering why. "Pierre
quit," she declared, as if that explained everything.

"Quit? Because of me?" Steve asked, suspecting
that he'd upset the other man that much. He seemed to
be very good at that today, and he didn't know why.

"Only partly," Kelly-Ann confessed. "Oh, it doesn't
matter why," she blurted. "I'm shorthanded and I
must get back to the shop!"

Steve grabbed her arm before she could stand again.
"Kelly-Ann, for pity's sake, settle down a minute and
let's think this out. I feel terrible."

She did, too. She really did. She was literally exhausted dealing with this man.

"Will it help if I call and apologize to Pierre?" Steve
asked.

"No!" she retorted, well aware that Pierre would be
even angrier if he heard from Steve.

Steve studied the problem. He did want to spend
more time with Kelly-Ann so he could get to know her.
He wanted that very much, without all this pressure
they both were clearly feeling.

Besides, he felt responsible for her misfortune in
losing her assistant. She'd said he was in part, though
he suspected he was wholly, to blame. Anyway, he
couldn't be with her if she had to spend all her time at
the shop catching up... Unless—

"I'll come help you!" he said impulsively.

"You?" she cried, stunned once more by his unpredictability. "You must be joking! What do you know about dog grooming?"

"A lot," he exaggerated.

After all, what could be so hard about it? He'd seen Jeffy groomed plenty of times. The trim might be a little tricky on some animals; still, he was confident he could pick that up in no time. He was a quick study.

Anyway, he had every intention of luring Pierre back to the shop somehow. He didn't mean to groom dogs for very long. He had his own work.

Most of all, he was feeling very sympathetic toward this woman he'd caused so much trouble. Sympathetic—and something else he couldn't label. Working with her might be the best solution for the time being.

"Don't you have a regular job?" she asked.

"Yes, but I've taken time off to be with Carlene," he explained. "To be honest, we're getting on each other's nerves at this stage. I need a distraction."

That was true on several counts, one of them being that he did need different stimuli to continue to be fresh for designing new computer programs.

"What do you do?" she asked.

"I work with software programs for corporations."

"You do?"

"Uh-huh."

"And you'll help me groom dogs?" Kelly-Ann asked, astonished.

"Yes," Steve replied enthusiastically. "When do I start?"

Kelly-Ann blanched. She hadn't been asking him to come. She'd been repeating a statement she found incredible. What made this man think he could groom dogs when he was used to creating software programs for computers?

Still—maybe she should see what stuff Steve Jamison was made of. She was betting he wouldn't last two hours.

"Well?" Steve prompted. "What time do I start?"

She looked at him in disbelief, trying to figure out what she'd gotten herself into.

"You're not going to vacillate, are you?" he teased, determined to pin her down. "You know you don't like that trait."

She shook her head, though she *was* undecided. "No," she fibbed. "Indecisiveness is not one of my traits." Big green eyes met deep brown ones. "And neither is criticizing and chattering," she couldn't help adding. "I'm not really like that, as you'll see when you get to know me."

He laughed again. "I'm sure you're not. I was reacting defensively when I made those charges. Anyway, I love to hear you talk. You must have been told this a thousand times, I'm sure, but I have to say it, too. You have the sweetest voice I've ever heard."

"I do?" she all but croaked, knowing her voice sounded anything but sweet at that moment.

No one had ever told her that. She'd always despised what she considered the little-girl quality of her voice, and when it got breathy because she was nervous, she was doubly embarrassed.

"Yes, you do," Steve said, brown eyes ablaze. He almost told her how beautiful her legs were. And her hair. And her body. But he decided that he was rushing things.

"Now when do you want me at the shop?"

"This evening at five-thirty," Kelly-Ann tried to say calmly, but her breathlessness betrayed her. This man had already said she was beautiful, and now he'd said her voice was the sweetest he'd ever heard. How would she ever work near him and not go crazy?

She cleared her throat and tried to sound business-like. "We'll probably have to work all evening to catch up. It will be an excellent initiation for you."

"Good," he said cheerfully, as if he really meant it. "Now that it's settled, let's have lunch. We have a busy schedule ahead of us, and I don't want to start a new job on an empty stomach."

Kelly-Ann could only sit and stare at him, dumb-founded. What had she done? What had he agreed to?

She really was crazy!

And so was he!

Maybe they were a matched pair.

Good grief! Only the stars knew what might happen!

Kelly-Ann felt as if she could touch the sky when Steve parked in the lot at the pet shop. They had settled down to normal conversation during a meal of fettuccini and hot, buttered garlic bread. She was very happy with both the warm, contented way the food—and Steve—made her feel.

Clearly a self-starter like she was, he'd achieved great success with his software programs, but obviously nothing induced him to neglect family. She'd found herself daydreaming again when he spoke of his devotion to his sister, despite Carlene being a difficult houseguest.

Kelly-Ann empathized with both the sixteen-year-old confined to home and the thirty-year-old man, who'd assumed the responsibility for her health and happiness. Kelly-Ann was eager to meet Carlene; she felt that they already shared a tie because of their love for animals—and, Kelly-Ann hoped, because of Steve.

She hadn't mentioned it to Steve. It was too soon, and anyway, she hadn't found the time to tell him about her pets—seven permanent ones and a host of strays. She and Steve had become absorbed in how to help Carlene through this unfortunate time and Jeffy's commercial prospects.

She'd listened as Steve had talked, and she'd learned some of the things she wanted to know. She was convinced he would be a wonderful husband and a great father—two characteristics high on her list for any man she might fall in love with.

The mere thought took her breath away. She hardly knew the man, and what she did know, she realized, were contrasts. He sounded as though he would be a good husband—if he could settle down. And he hadn't made any mention of doing that.

How easily she could deceive herself with Steve Jamison! She wanted to believe he could fit into her life, that he could be the companion she wanted, the lover, the— There she went again.

Steve's next comment brought her abruptly back to reality. "I haven't bored you, I hope, Kelly-Ann. I didn't realize until I stopped the car how much I dominated the conversation during lunch. I'm sorry. It's really not like me."

She smiled. "I had a wonderful time, Steve. I enjoyed hearing about your business and your sister."

He reached out and clasped her hand. Kelly-Ann watched in helpless anticipation as he drew it to his lips and kissed it with all the chivalry of a romantic lover.

"You're very gracious," he murmured against her fingers, sending shivers up and down her spine. "During dinner, I promise to give you a chance to talk about anything on your mind. Even," he said, his brown eyes twinkling again, "your penchant to read an animal's horoscope. That really was interesting about Jeffy."

"Oh, but animals have horoscopes just like humans," she said seriously. "They're born under the same set of circumstances that we are. In fact, some people choose their pets according to the animal's sun sign...."

She let the words trail off. Enough about that, for crying out loud! His eyes were laughing, and she didn't want to think that he thought she was crazy. She'd had a wonderful time and she wanted to leave it at that.

"I'll see you at five-thirty," he said. "We'll talk more about animals then."

Kelly-Ann had forgotten about that. "Really, Steve, I don't think that's the best idea," she murmured, feeling uncertain all over again.

"We agreed," he said, as if that settled the matter.

And, indeed, they had. But to what?

"We'll work, and then we'll change clothes and go to this superb little Mexican restaurant I know about. You do like Mexican food, don't you?"

"Yes, I do. I really do!" she added for emphasis, "but, Steve, I don't have time for dinner."

She was feeling guilty again. After all, she'd refused to have dinner with Ted, and she and Steve had just gone to lunch.

"You'll need dinner," he said easily, "the same as you needed lunch. Don't you feel better?"

"Yes," she reluctantly agreed. "Yes, I do."

She really felt wonderful. Still, they would be working late, if he proved any help at all, and she would be tired. Even contemplating dinner wore her out!

"I think we should forget dinner tonight," she said. "You're going to find out that grooming pets is tedious physical work, regardless of how much you love animals or how good the creatures are. And, anyway," she added almost ruefully, "I'm finishing up the biggies tonight."

"The biggies?"

"The big dogs. Like Horace, the one Pierre and I were doing when you came in this morning."

"Uh-huh," Steve said, wishing he didn't remember. "Horace the horse."

Kelly-Ann nodded. "He's the one." Solemn green eyes met doubting brown. "It's not too late to say no," she suggested.

She didn't know how she would manage without help, now that she herself was reminded of what she faced, yet she couldn't see this computer programmer handling hundred-pound dogs.

Steve broke into a big smile. "Of course, I'm not going to say no. If a pretty little lady like you can manage the Horaces of the pet world, then I'm sure I can."

Kelly-Ann giggled, the tinkling sound merrily filling the car. Steve Jamison had a surprise in store. The

Horaces of the world could be backbreaking, hernia-inducing, ear-splitting trouble when they tried.

She'd let him find that out on his own, since he was so insistent. Besides, it was important to her that he know something about her work. Very important.

"All right, but don't say I didn't warn you," she said.

He nodded. "Forewarned and forearmed."

Anyway, Steve told himself, if Pierre could handle those humongous beasts, so could he. He was almost twice the other man's size. But he didn't want to think about poor Pierre now. That was why he was in this position, for better or worse.

"You'll definitely see me at five-thirty," he said, getting out of the car.

"You don't need to walk me in," Kelly-Ann said.

Steve smiled. "That may be; however, if I don't pick up Jeffy, Carlene will throw a fit. In fact," he said, "I should have called her, but I want to tell her about the commercial possibility in person."

"Oh, yes, Jeffy, of course," Kelly-Ann said, feeling foolish again. She'd forgotten Jeffy! This man must wonder how she conducted business at all.

As they walked toward the pet shop, Steve wrapped his arm around her. Kelly-Ann instantly forgot not only Jeffy, but how silly she'd felt. She dared not add further comment for fear of making the situation worse.

Chapter Eight

Kelly-Ann was beside herself with anticipation by the time five-thirty came. Lisa would be working until six, and Kelly-Ann almost wished the young girl wasn't there. That was totally insane, of course, because she needed Lisa's assistance.

She hadn't told her helper that Steve was coming. She wasn't sure why. Was it because she was afraid he wouldn't come? Or that he would?

Oh, for pity's sake! She didn't want to think about it anymore. But her gaze went again and again to the clock that had ticked slowly since her return at four. Heaven knew she and Lisa had been busy, yet time had dragged.

She jumped nervously when the bell sounded at the front desk. Glancing over the café door, she saw Steve grinning.

"I'm only a little sorry for startling you again," he said, his voice playful. "I couldn't resist. I wanted you to remember this morning because I'm going to make up for it tonight."

Drawing in a steadying breath, Kelly-Ann asked herself just what it was he was going to make up for—and how. She forced a smile.

"You bet you are. Come on back and grab an apron." She pointed to a cage behind her. "I've been saving Sadie for you."

If Steve had been made of less stern stuff, he would have blanched. "Sadie, huh?" he said with pretended carelessness, looking at the huge, shaggy dog in the pen. "She favors Horace."

Kelly-Ann laughed aloud. She honestly had been saving Sadie for Steve. She had tried to bathe the dog earlier, but had wrestled with her in vain. In fact, she didn't know what she was going to do; she didn't believe Steve would have any success, either. More than one time, she'd mourned the loss of Pierre, who was amazingly adept with the animals.

When Lisa heard Steve, she rushed from the rear of the shop where she'd put a freshly groomed Doberman in a cage. "Oh, wow!" she cried. "Steve! The *big* man! Are you going to help me do Sadie?"

Casting a furtive glance at the teenager, Kelly-Ann found Lisa lit up like a light bulb again.

Steve winked at the girl. "I'm going to help somebody. Are you bathing Sadie with me?" He looked at Kelly-Ann, his grin broadening. "Or do you get the honors?"

Kelly-Ann arched her eyebrows and put her hands on her hips. Now this was going to be something to see!

She would let Lisa and Steve have a go at Sadie. His arrogance and her eagerness should prove eventful. The half Lab, half wolfhound was sneaky and stubborn.

"Let me do it!" Lisa cried. "Let Steve help me."

Kelly-Ann had to smile at the girl's determination. And, after all, she couldn't blame Lisa for being smitten by Steve. She was, too!

"All right. Give it a try, but I'm going to be truthful. I'll bet Sadie gives you a fit. I don't think you two can manage her."

"Oh, you don't!" Steve taunted. "Well, pretty lady, you're on. A kiss is on the line! I say Lisa and I will do fine. If we win the bet, you owe me a kiss."

Kelly-Ann stared at him, her gaze going automatically to his gorgeous mouth. She *wanted* a kiss from Steve Jamison! Still, she couldn't admit that. Although she wasn't one for gambling, she would play his game—and hope he won!

Green eyes sparkling at the mere thought, she agreed. "I'll take that bet, mister."

When Lisa looked at Kelly-Ann, the woman's face turned crimson. "Well, go on," she coaxed, motioning to the girl. "Get Sadie."

Confident, Lisa went to the cage and led Sadie out. The dog seemed docile enough, and Kelly-Ann watched with mixed emotions as Steve refused the apron she offered. He was dressed much too enticingly in jeans, a pullover shirt and tennis shoes. He was sure to get soaked to the skin.

Grinning, Lisa walked the dog to the bathing area. At the edge of the tub, which sat about two feet off the floor with a ramp leading up to it, Sadie balked. In fact, she stopped dead in her tracks.

Steve glanced at Kelly-Ann. Lisa pulled on the harness to no avail. Steve ingenuously decided to push the animal from the rear. Sadie promptly turned around and snapped at him, causing him to jerk back.

Kelly-Ann emitted an inadvertent giggle, although she was disappointed she wasn't going to get to kiss Steve. "Okay, I think I've proved my point. I'll take care of Sadie. Lisa, take out P. S. Poodle and initiate Steve in the art of trimming."

"Wait!" Steve insisted. "I'm not through with Sadie yet. Give me a minute here."

Kelly-Ann shook her head. "Trust me. She's through with you. I'll handle her. Or at least, I'll try."

"Hold it," Steve insisted. "I need to give this some thought."

Shaking her head, Kelly-Ann was adamant. "It won't do any good. I don't think she likes you. She never tried to bite anyone before."

"Hey, you're trying to hurt my feelings," Steve joked. "The problem was that I didn't give her any respect. After all, I did put my hands where they obviously didn't belong." He snapped his fingers. "Ah, ha! I haven't been foiled yet! An idea is in the making. Hold on here. I'll be right back."

Kelly-Ann watched in amusement as he vanished out the front door. In minutes, he'd returned with something in a paper bag.

"Now, you wait!" she exclaimed. "What do you have? Please don't do anything rash."

"No way," he said. "But watch this ingenuity from a man who thinks up clever things all the time."

Kelly-Ann watched cautiously as he pulled a dog chewie from the bag and held it out to Sadie. Lisa could hardly hang on to the leash when Sadie saw what Steve had. When she reached it, he only let her sniff it, then led her toward the tub again. Holding the chewie away from her, he encouraged the dog to walk up the ramp.

When she did, he tricked her into the tub. "Ta-dah!" he said smugly. "And how would you have gotten her in there, Kelly-Ann?"

"Pierre . . ." she let the word trail away. "It depends upon the animal. Some go willingly. Others can be coaxed. Still others have to literally be lifted. Animals do have great dignity. In fact, you were right about insulting Sadie by pushing on her."

Steve became pensive for a moment. He wasn't into animal psychology; however, he didn't want to insult Kelly-Ann by commenting. Besides, as he looked around the shop, he began to think of ways to improve it, to streamline it for efficiency.

"You know, what you need is a hydraulic lift of some kind that would raise and lower the tub. Maybe you could get a better system—sort of like a car wash."

Kelly-Ann smiled. "Yes, a hydraulic lift might be efficient, Steve. It really could be an idea that would work with proper plumbing, but please remember that those are living creatures. They need love and care, the personal touch—not an assembly line like a car wash."

Steve's face turned red. Of course, animals weren't automobiles to be washed and wiped dry. He hadn't thought about what he was saying; he'd been so busy trying to think of a way to organize the bathing that he'd ignored the human element.

"You're right, naturally," he murmured, feeling insensitive.

She grinned. "I'm glad you agree, and now, that point aside, just how do you propose to wash Sadie with our present setup?"

"What do you mean?" he asked, peering at the dog.

He saw that she was down on the floor of the tub, totally engrossed in gnawing on the treat that he had carried in the car for Jeffy.

Steve groaned. "I hadn't thought that far."

Kelly-Ann laughed again. "In this case, as in all others, you do what you can. Work around her." She winked at him. "To tell you the truth, the chewie wasn't the best idea."

He shook his head. "I guess not. My method doesn't invalidate the bet, does it? I did get her in there."

Kelly-Ann felt her heart skip a beat. Was he joking? She wanted that kiss! Still, she couldn't say that.

"I guess you did, if you count the bottom line," she said.

"Great!" he declared, his glittering gaze holding hers. "When do I get to collect?" His voice dropped an octave.

The color crept up Kelly-Ann's neck as she looked at Lisa, who watched the couple with obvious fascination. Steve followed Kelly-Ann's eyes.

He looked back at her. "You know I'm teasing about the kiss. I just wanted to make proving my point more interesting. Now I'm ready to work."

"I want to work with him," Lisa pleaded.

Kelly-Ann struggled to suppress her disappointment. Thank the stars above she hadn't let on how much she'd wanted that kiss! She thought it was pos-

sibly best that Lisa worked with this enticing man tonight.

"All right, Lisa, but bathe *all* of the dog, please.
You'll have to coax her into a standing position and
leash her somehow."

Lisa looked at Steve. He looked at Kelly-Ann. She
managed a smile, then escaped toward P.S. She had to
get a grip on reality, even if it was in the form of a dog!

"By the way," she called over her shoulder, having
forgotten in the excitement of Steve's being there,
"what did Carlene say about Jeffy's commercial possibilities?"

Steve's brown eyes glowed as he straightened up.
"She was delighted! She's eager to get back into ther-
apy so her leg will heal quicker. The news was a good
boost for both of us."

Kelly-Ann glanced at the tub in time to see Sadie
adroitly leap over the side, chewie still in her mouth.

"You were supposed to hang on to her until I leashed
her!" Lisa sputtered, staring accusingly at Steve as Sadie bolted toward the front of the shop.

"Oh, hell!" Steve groaned, a reenactment of
Horace's adventures surging into his mind.

Kelly-Ann went after the errant animal. What else
was there to do?

At six o'clock, Lisa was more than eager to leave. In
the bathing of Sadie, somehow the thrill of Steve had
apparently worn thin.

Kelly-Ann had heard the grunts and groans—and
snarls—as Sadie resisted to the bitter end. Kelly-Ann
had an idea the dog must have finished her treat before she allowed Steve and Lisa to finish her bath.

The girl looked wet and exhausted when she came back to tell Kelly-Ann she was leaving. "I'll see you on Monday," Lisa said.

"Are you sure you don't want to come in just this one Saturday and help me out?" Kelly-Ann asked hopefully.

Lisa shook her head. "No way. I should get overtime for bathing Sadie. What a trip!"

Kelly-Ann didn't remind the girl that she'd begged to bathe the dog, with Steve's help, of course. She wasn't at all surprised when Lisa leaned nearer and murmured, "Good luck with the big man. I think you're going to need it. He's—er—not all that good with animals."

Kelly-Ann smiled. She hadn't thought he would be; still, he looked so appealing, standing there by the tub, obviously proud of the job he'd done, and soaked to the skin. She couldn't help noticing the way his jeans and shirt clung damply to his male form.

"He'll learn," she said lightly, though she really didn't think he'd work that long.

"Well, *you* teach him," Lisa whispered. "I mean," she added, "he's a hunk and all that, but he's no Pierre in the animal department, if you know what I'm hinting at."

Kelly-Ann giggled, causing Steve to glance at her. She knew what Lisa meant, all right.

"What's so funny?" Steve asked, coming toward them.

"I'm out of here," Lisa said, managing a smile for Steve in spite of her disillusionment with the man.

"Lisa, please don't forget to stop by my house," Kelly-Ann reminded the girl.

"I never do," she tossed over her shoulder.

Steve walked over to Kelly-Ann. "Okay, what's so funny?" he repeated.

Smiling broadly, she said, "We could start with you. Look how drenched you are!"

He laughed, and she was pleased to see he had a sense of humor. "Give me a break. So, we both took a bath. I'm still learning. And speaking of breaks," he added, bending forward, "my back feels like it will."

"It hurts worst the first day," Kelly-Ann said. "You get used to it."

No way, Steve told himself. He would never get used to it. He'd have to find a way to lure Pierre back. This woman needed the Frenchman. Steve would talk to Suzette about it, but for now, he was committed to the job of assisting with these beasts Kelly-Ann called dogs.

"Who's next?" he asked, pretending enthusiasm for the chore.

Kelly-Ann arched her eyebrows, slowly turned around and pointed to an overweight, decrepit hound.

"You're kidding," Steve said, the enthusiasm completely gone from his voice. "Does that one even walk?"

When Kelly-Ann laughed merrily, Steve smiled. He loved that happy sound her voice made.

"She walks, but she doesn't leap," the dog groomer said. "We have to lift her into the tub."

"Oh, my aching back," Steve groaned.

"Exactly," she agreed. "Mine, too. At least we can take our time now. All the owners who insisted upon picking up their pets today have claimed them."

"That's a relief," Steve said. "Well, we may as well get on with it. What's this one's name?"

"Cleopatra," Kelly-Ann said with a giggle.

They had just succeeded in getting the heavy animal into the tub when the phone rang. "Hold on to her leash," Kelly-Ann cautioned.

"Don't worry," Steve assured her. "I've learned my lesson. Cleopatra isn't going anywhere."

"Hello," Kelly-Ann answered breathlessly when she'd raced to the phone in the reception room.

"Kelly-Ann, it's Ted," the eye doctor announced. "It's dinnertime and I thought perhaps you'd changed your mind by now. I really want to see you."

A flush of guilt colored Kelly-Ann's face. She glanced back at Steve, knowing that he'd insisted they share dinner tonight.

"I—I'm still bathing dogs," she murmured. "I'm sorry. I told you I'd have to work late."

"You still have to eat," he said pleasantly. "You know how you love the fettucini at our Italian place."

Kelly-Ann's face turned crimson. "I'm sorry. I can't, Ted," she said firmly.

There was a brief pause, then he said, "Well, don't say I didn't try. I'll think about you when I bite into that delicious pasta and sip a glass of red wine."

Fresh memories of lunch with Steve rushed to Kelly-Ann's mind. And she would be here thinking only of Steve while Ted was thinking of her! Oh, what a day this had turned out to be! She didn't know what else to say to the man she'd been so enamored with until this very morning!

"Kelly-Ann—"

She realized he was still trying to coax her, to tempt her, and usually it would have worked. Easily.

"Thanks for thinking of me," she murmured. Then she made herself say, "I know you hate to eat alone, Ted. Why don't you invite someone else?"

She bit down on her lip as she waited for his response. She couldn't believe she was trying to get rid of Ted Haffner, and after she'd worked so hard for so long to make him hers!

It was incredible. She glanced back at Steve. Their eyes met as he firmly held on to Cleopatra. Where, oh, where would this all lead? Kelly-Ann asked herself. Why was she allowing this man, this unreliable Pisces, to submerge her world in total chaos?

She knew the answer: she had no choice. For better or worse, Steve Jamison had stepped into her life and changed it. Now only fate knew what was in store for her.

Fate, and perhaps Steve.

By nine o'clock, all the big dogs had been done, Steve was soaking wet and Kelly-Ann was a mess.

"We're finally finished," she announced as she closed the door on the last cage.

"Thank God," Steve muttered. He was hunkered down on the floor, looking wonderfully masculine and woefully wiped out and wet.

Kelly-Ann laughed. "How did you like your first time grooming dogs?"

Steve frowned, then laughed aloud. "I don't intend to give up my day job," he joked.

She smiled. "I didn't think you did."

They were silent for a moment, each lost in thought. Kelly-Ann told herself that she could get used to having Steve around, full-time, in any capacity. He had learned quickly and he was clever.

"You did a good job," she said softly. "I, of all people, know what hard work it is. Still, I love it."

His face gentled as he looked at her. "And you're very, very good with the animals. They love you."

Kelly-Ann was uncomfortable. They were using the word *love* so lightly, and each time it was mentioned, something triggered in her mind. She tried to catch herself before she could drift off into fantasyland.

"Listen, I truly think it's time we called it a day," she said. "We're completely exhausted. I do appreciate your help, but I don't expect you to come again to do this. I've bathed all the big animals. I'll work tomorrow to catch up on the smaller ones, then Monday, Suzette and I switch shops."

"Hold it!" Steve insisted. "You're not getting rid of me that easily." He stood up, then groaned as he grabbed his back with both hands.

"Are you all right?" she asked anxiously, moving closer.

He looked down at her. "I'm fine. It's just my back that's broken."

"I'm sorry," she murmured, concerned. "Why don't I drive you home? We can make arrangements to get your car to you tomorrow. I do know how painful a sore back can be. What you need to do is soak in a hot—"

He winked at her as he finished the sentence. "*Tub*. And that's exactly what I intend to do. My club is open until eleven. We'll *both* soak in a Jacuzzi."

"Your *club?*"

"Yes, I belong to a private club, and I can bring guests. Have you ever relaxed in a Jacuzzi with all that warm water swirling around you, soothing aching muscles?" he asked.

"No, and I can't now," she said hurriedly, although the idea sounded daringly appealing.

"Nonsense," he declared. "We're going to dinner tonight, remember, at a Mexican restaurant, which, by the way, is open until midnight. We'll have time to do it all."

Kelly-Ann wasn't sure what *all* of it was, but those darned alarms went off in her head again. She'd seen too much of this man today. Much too much.

"I'm too beat, honestly," she hedged. "I'll give you a rain check on dinner."

"Feel these corded muscles," Steve said, pulling her nearer. Her hands trembled as he placed them on his back. "I've got to get in that Jacuzzi, and I insist that you join me—*before* dinner. After all, you're planning to go home and get in a tub of hot water to relax, aren't you?"

Kelly-Ann nodded. She was. That was true. But she was planning to do it alone.

"Right," he announced. "I knew that. So, here's the schedule. We'll stop by your place, pick up a swimsuit and change of clothes, go by mine, get me a suit and change of clothes, go to the club, then have dinner. Now, doesn't that sound good?''

Kelly-Ann looked up into mesmerizing brown eyes as Steve continued to hold her hands, using his own to ensure that she caressed his taut muscles.

''Yes,'' she whispered.

What else could she possibly say?

Chapter Nine

Kelly-Ann couldn't contain her excitement as she drove to her house on the outskirts of town, with Steve following in his car. The weariness she'd felt moments ago had melted in the heat of his brown eyes when she'd agreed to go to his club.

Her mind raced frantically over her clothing possibilities. She knew the Mexican restaurant he was speaking of; she had something to wear there. What really bothered her was the matter of the bathing suit.

She wanted so much for Steve Jamison to find her attractive in every way; she needed to shower and do something with her hair. She would have to make some excuse to do that quickly while he waited for her.

Worse, she hadn't cleaned her house. Although she had picked up the clutter somewhat, with three dogs and four cats, inevitably there would be hair everywhere. When she knew in advance someone was coming, she vacuumed the furniture. Steve needed to change clothes anyway. Still...

Driving behind Kelly-Ann, Steve thought about what an amazing day they'd shared, from 9:00 a.m. to 9:00 p.m., and he was sure the most interesting part was yet to come.

He liked crazy Kelly-Ann Keernan, this woman with the Cancer sun sign, with her grooming shop and her sweet voice, with her dimples and her pretty legs. He liked her exceptionally well, and surprisingly, he'd enjoyed the time bathing animals with her. She was totally unpretentious and naturally loving. And it had been evident when she worked with the dogs.

He frowned as she switched on her right-turn signal to turn onto a street four over from the one he himself lived on. Did she live in his neighborhood? He thought she'd said something about owning a house, and his area was exclusive condominiums.

When they drove toward the shop where Suzette had been working today, K.K.'s Number One Pet Perfections, Steve thought Kelly-Ann must be going there, but he was wrong. She gave another right-turn signal and continued down the next street, three from his own, than made a left turn and went all the way to the end of that street, the one that intersected the street he lived on!

Incredibly, she drove down that street to the end, gave a left-turn signal and turned onto the street that backed on to his. He couldn't imagine where she lived.

There was only one old rambling house where the road dead-ended, a house that the tenants in his own building constantly complained about, a house where a loony woman lived among hordes of annoying animals.

Slowly but surely, Steve began to draw parallels in his mind. Kelly-Ann *couldn't* be that woman, could she? He himself had phoned several times to complain about that zoo on the property. He'd even called the officials about the noise the dogs often made, the yowling of cats in the middle of the night, and other assorted strange sounds.

He'd been told that nothing could be done since both he and the woman were in the county where there were no zoning restrictions, and even if there had been, she would have been given a variance for her hundred-year-old house.

Steve's heart began to hammer as his worst fears were confirmed. Kelly-Ann gave another signal and drove down the winding gravel drive to that awful sprawling old house that housed all those animals. *She* was the woman!

All smiles, Kelly-Ann hopped out of her car and walked back to Steve's. "Now remember that *you* insisted on dinner tonight," she said, although she was clearly happy he had. "My place is a mess, and so am I. I need a few minutes to get things together."

Steve nodded as he walked with her toward the house. Kelly-Ann *was* the loony woman! He didn't know why it stunned him so.

Perhaps he should have recognized that sweet voice, but he hadn't thought of it as sweet when he heard it responding to his complaints on the other end of the phone. Of course, it all added up: she was the kind of woman who would live here so that she could have all those barking, yipping, yowling, howling pets!

"Steve," she murmured as she opened the gate to the picket fence, "is something wrong?" Fortunately—or unfortunately—she was already sensitive to his moods.

He smiled down at her. "No, of course not."

"You're so quiet," she observed.

He didn't like her home, she told herself unhappily. He was displeased already, before he entered.

She looked at the old house with the climbing wild-rose bushes just beginning to bloom, the daffodils that would be yellow and beautiful by daylight, the dogwood trees exquisite with their budding pink flowers, and the huge lilac bushes with their sweet smell.

In the dim spring moonlight, it was impossible to see all the beauty she saw. The old house had heart, atmosphere, character. But perhaps Steve Jamison didn't like all those things. Maybe only a silly, sentimental female as she was, a daydreamer, could appreciate the coziness of the place, the possibilities, the promise and the past.

Naturally, Kelly-Ann had the advantage, having spent her entire life here, as had her mother and grandmother before her. This was the house she'd always wanted to fill with the sounds of happy children and animals.

She had had dozens of imaginary playmates when she was growing up, but she'd had no brothers or sisters and no little friends who lived nearby. This was a wonderful place for children—a huge old house, a big yard with room to run and play.

Still, she felt that Steve didn't care for what he was seeing at all. She sensed his displeasure, as if he were contemptuous of her for her home, of all things. Con-

temptuous and condemning as he had been this morning.

Dispirited, Kelly-Ann walked up on the porch. Two
cats ran toward her, mewing gently. Lisa must have let
them out at six when she stopped by.

Steve watched as the woman picked up both cats and
cuddled them. Minutes ago, he had found her love for
animals charming, indicative of the depth of caring she
was capable of.

Now he could only think of their contrasting life-
styles. Although, ironically, he literally lived two
hundred feet from her, they were miles apart in all the
ways that counted. He didn't care what horoscopes and
stars and sun signs said. He and Kelly-Ann Keernan
were like two people inhabiting separate planets.

His home was a contemporary condominium with
nothing out of place, including the yard. A gardener
came twice a month to make sure that everything
looked as it should: pruned and clipped and neat.
There were no wild, rambling, untrained plants in his
yard. Nor was there a porch to be cluttered with animals and furniture as this one was.

The inside was as tidy as the outside. Or, rather, it
had been, until Carlene and Jeffy had invaded the
premises. Now there was occasional disorder, but
this—

Abruptly someone walked around from the backyard. Kelly-Ann gasped, and Steve found himself
poised for battle.

"Excuse me," Pierre said sullenly. "I came to care
for the bunny, but I see I am here at the bad time."

"No!" Steve insisted too quickly and too vehe-
mently. "I mean," he amended, "I, myself, am happy

to see you, Pierre." After all, he had no right to speak for Kelly-Ann.

"You?" the Frenchman challenged. "Happy to see *me?*"

"Yes, indeed," Steve said smoothly. "I owe you an apology, and I'm glad for the opportunity to make it. I shouldn't have gone into the back of the shop and I shouldn't have grabbed you."

Kelly-Ann breathed a sigh of relief. She hadn't known what to expect when she realized Pierre was the one approaching them. She still didn't know what to expect from him, but she was pleased to see him and grateful Steve had made the first move.

"I'm happy to see you, too, Pierre," she said sincerely. "I missed you today. I wish you would come back to work."

Even in the scant light, she could see Pierre puff up proudly.

"Well," he said, pensively, "I am the one wronged, but I am a big man. I allow the apologies." He turned to Steve. "And I say to you that there is the chance I acted too quitly—I mean *quickly.*"

"Thank you, Pierre," Kelly-Ann said softly. "I hope this means you'll come back to work." She glanced at Steve. "I'm afraid Mr. Jamison doesn't possess the talent you do with animals."

Steve smiled. He didn't. He was sure of that.

Pierre smiled broadly. "I accept the job, also. Now, I bid you *adieu!*"

"Goodbye," Kelly-Ann and Steve said in unison.

Kelly-Ann wasn't about to push her luck by asking Pierre to return to help her on Saturday. She would manage.

She and Steve remained silent as Pierre left, then Kelly-Ann put the two cats down and searched her purse for house keys.

"Boy, I'm glad that's resolved," she said with a sigh of relief. "I really do need Pierre."

"Yes," Steve agreed. "You do. I'm glad it's resolved, too."

Kelly-Ann laughed softly. "Poor man. You did have to work hard tonight, didn't you?"

Steve nodded. "It was definitely an experience."

One he didn't want to repeat. He was truly grateful that Pierre had shown up, although now he had time to ponder the man's comment about the bunny. Good heavens, did the woman have rabbits here, too?

Kelly-Ann started apologizing for the house the moment she opened the door. "I didn't expect company, so I didn't clean," she said nervously. "And some of the poor animals were abused, so they sometimes make mistakes."

She shut up abruptly. She was determined not to ramble, not to be put on the defensive. If Steve didn't like her and her house and her charity work, then so be it.

Even as she made the bold statement to herself, she wished it not to be so. She *wanted* him to like her, her house and her animals. She wanted it very much.

Gazing around the room in amazement as animals rushed from all over the place to greet Kelly-Ann, Steve didn't know what to think, what to say.

"These are the regulars," Kelly-Ann said softly, pointing out three dogs and four cats, whom she called by name. "Those," she indicated a scruffy parrot in a cage, another small dog and two more cats, "are my charity work, boarders looking for new homes."

"What happened to their old ones?" Steve managed to ask.

Her bright green eyes became sad instantly, as if he'd touched her soul with the simple question. "Their owners tossed them out on the street, literally, or left them at the shop or at my veterinarian's shop. Oh, I just hate that!" she exclaimed passionately. "I hate it when people throw away these precious, loving, helpless animals like toys they've grown bored with!"

Steve drew in a deep breath as he stared at her blazing green eyes and her animated face. She was passionate and concerned. She was loving and nurturing.

But she wasn't for him.

Although he was glad someone cared about neglected animals, glad that someone championed their cause, glad that someone gave them a home, that kind of person wasn't someone who would fit into his orderly world of computer chips and disk storage and business meetings.

When Steve didn't comment, Kelly-Ann grew quiet again. She knew that some people were overwhelmed when they first saw her home with its castaways, some of whom could be very naughty and do things like claw chair backs and chew the old mahogany furniture legs.

Most people, people with a heart themselves, accepted the disarray and disorder and understood that a way station for refugees of any kind would be rumpled and worn by the transients.

Would Steve?

She glanced at him and the sadness deepened inside her. "If you'll excuse me, I'll only be a moment or two," she said, not knowing what else to say. "I'll—er—I'll just take a quick shower and get my swim-suit."

After he didn't acknowledge her a second time, something stubborn and willful inside made Kelly-Ann slowly turn to face him, whether she wanted to or not.

"That is, if you still want me to share the rest of the evening with you," she said tightly, wishing it didn't matter so much.

"Yes, of course," he replied quickly.

He certainly couldn't say he *didn't* after he'd been so insistent. Besides, he *thought* he still did want her to.

He met those green eyes of hers. "Yes," he repeated more firmly, wondering who he was trying to convince, him or her. "I want you to."

But, dear Lord in heaven, what then? He stared in amazement as she rushed away. So, this was her *charity* work, as she referred to it. All these miserable animals. He looked from one to the other.

They didn't exactly look miserable, he conceded. In fact, they appeared amazingly healthy, happy and well-behaved.

He stroked his jaw as he pondered the racket they made that disturbed everyone in his building. And the surrounding buildings, he felt obligated to add. Perhaps the new arrivals created a ruckus until Kelly-Ann got them in hand or found homes for them.

Scanning the room, he saw afresh the woman's warmth and homeyness. The house was reasonably neat, with the exception of the puffs of dog and cat hair to be seen here and there, on the furniture and floor. There were huge plants everywhere. He walked over to the fireplace to look at some old framed photographs and noticed that the mantelpiece had been chewed on.

"Geez!" he muttered. "What on earth did that?"

As if to provide an answer, the parrot squawked loudly. Steve spun around. Kelly-Ann, no doubt, let the bird fly free to exercise. The mantel would be an excellent perch.

As he heard Kelly-Ann turn on the shower, he exhaled slowly. She had been right. They had had a long day. He shouldn't have invited her out tonight. He wished he hadn't come here, hadn't seen with his own eyes why they could never be compatible, no matter what their sun signs said.

He could never live this way. It was inconceivable to him. It was...was distasteful. There, he'd admitted it. The messy animals, the clutter, the noise.

At least it all made sense to him now. Of course, this woman would live this way. Her pet shops were a way of life, and this was a natural by-product of her love for animals.

What was she to do when faced with abandoned animals? Oh, hell, he didn't want to think about it.

He sat down on the sagging couch and put his head in his hands. One of the "regulars" ambled up to him and nuzzled his knee. He looked into a pair of big brown eyes, loving, warm, concerned eyes. The old dog gazed at him as if in empathy for the predicament Steve found himself in—intrigued by a woman totally out of his realm.

He stood up abruptly. What on earth was he doing thinking the damned dog was commiserating with him?

And why was he questioning everything about his existence, his way of life, his choices, since he met the nutty woman with the water sign? He was surprised she didn't have fish here.

He'd no sooner thought it than he was distracted by a sound in the long, wide hall. He dared to investigate.

And there it was: a huge aquarium filled with fish. He did a double take when he saw a big, fat gray cat sitting on the corners of the tank, batting at the fish nearest the top of the water.

"Get away from there!" he told the lethargic creature. "Get away!"

When the cat looked at him as if he'd lost his mind, Steve pushed at him. The animal lost his balance a bit, but quickly resettled himself.

"Kelly-Ann!" Steve called.

Abruptly, she turned up in the hall. He didn't even see which room she appeared from.

"What?" she cried, hearing the anxiety in his voice.

"Look at this cat!" he demanded. "He's after the fish."

Kelly-Ann giggled. Somehow she hadn't expected Steve to be worried about the fish in her aquarium when he called her name so unexpectedly.

"Toby won't hurt them," she said. "He's just entertaining himself, and see—" she pointed at the fish swimming around in circles at the top "—they're not afraid."

He looked at her in amazement. "What the hell am I doing here worrying about fish?" he asked as much for his own benefit as hers.

Her dimples showed, and her voice was sweet when she spoke. "Naturally, you're worried about the fish. You're a water sign. I'm glad you're concerned, Steve.

You seemed...contemptuous when you saw how I live.''

He was taken aback by her perceptiveness. He wanted to deny the observation. Unfortunately, *contempt* was a good word for what he'd felt when he realized who she was and what a problem she'd been to the neighborhood.

Now as he looked into her eyes, he didn't know what to say. He wasn't going to lie to her, though he wasn't going to hurt her, either. For the first time, he noticed that she was wrapped in a towel. His gaze unconsciously skimmed over her.

She was extraordinarily pretty in a wholesome way. Her wavy dark hair hung damply down her back. She didn't have her glasses on; her green eyes were huge and dreamy. And those legs...those incredible Kelly-Ann legs...

"You'd better get dressed," he murmured. "We don't want to be too late for the club."

She seemed as shocked as he to realize she was in a towel. "I'm sorry!" she exclaimed. "When you called, you sounded so alarmed."

He laughed. "I can't believe it myself, but I was worried about those damned fish. And the cat wouldn't move. I tried to get him off the tank."

She giggled. "Thank you, Steve Jamison, for worrying about my pets."

Then she turned on her heel and vanished into a room.

Steve stared after her, shaking his head.

"Steve Jamison," he murmured. "What are you doing? What on God's earth are you doing?"

He didn't know. What he did know for certain now was that he wanted to do it: he wanted to take Kelly-Ann to the club and to dinner.

And then?

Only heaven knew.

Chapter Ten

When Kelly-Ann came back to the living room, Steve was watching the antics of the beautifully colored Amazon parrot.

"Does he talk?" he asked, glancing at the woman.

She had dressed in a green-and-blue muumuu, and his gaze went to it immediately. The colors caused her eyes to look more emerald and her hair to look darker. She had braided it in a single plait, and Steve could see that it was still damp from the shower.

"I've got my swimsuit on under this," she said. "I thought I could wear the dress to the restaurant after we're through at the club." She gestured to her purse. "I have my unmentionables in here."

He grinned at her. "Your unmentionables?"

She blushed charmingly. "You know, my—"

"Yes," he said. "I do know. You just look so pretty when you turn pink."

"Oh, Steve, you're awful!" she protested. "After the day we've had, how can you still tease?"

"It's easy," he confessed with a lazy smile.

"Easy does it!" the parrot suddenly squawked, startling Steve.

Kelly-Ann laughed. "You're nervous, Mr. Jamison. And, yes, the parrot does talk."

"I figured that out," he said, winking at her. He went nearer to the cage.

"And he bites," she warned.

"He bites, he bites, he bites," the bird echoed.

Steve seemed fascinated. "He talks well. I've never heard a parrot talk. I mean a real one." He looked at her and shook his head. "What I *really* mean is, a parrot I've seen in person. Of course, I've seen them talking on television."

She smiled. "I knew what you meant, Steve."

"Yes," he said. "Of course, you did."

"Yes!" the parrot screamed. "Yes!"

"How big is his vocabulary?" Steve asked.

Kelly-Ann shrugged. "I'm not sure. I suppose I've heard about fifty different words."

"How long have you had him?"

She sighed. "Long enough. He's delightful to watch from a distance, but he's a bronco, meaning that he's been mistreated. He doesn't trust anyone. I'm having an awful time placing him." She smiled winningly. "Wouldn't you like to have him?"

Steve shook his head. "No way. Jeffy and Carlene are enough for me." He took her elbow. "Let's get out of here before you try to talk me into a cat."

Sighing softly again, Kelly-Ann went with him, but she found herself wishing she'd been able to talk him into *any* of the animals. She would have seen it as a positive sign. His adamant refusal left her feeling down. She knew she could never care for a man who didn't have compassion for his fellow creatures.

She glanced at Steve as he guided her to his car, his hand still on her elbow. There was just one more problem: she was afraid she cared for him already.

When Steve turned onto the next street over and drove down to the end, Kelly-Ann stared at him in amazement. "Do you live in these condominiums?"

He nodded.

She was flabbergasted. "No!"

"Yes."

"Oh, you wouldn't believe the meanie who owns the building over there," she said, pointing to the one at the end of a long row. Then she watched in disbelief as Steve drove right to that one.

She stared in surprise when he used a remote-control unit to raise the garage door of a two-story, four-unit condo.

"Your building?" she all but whispered.

He nodded. "My building."

Kelly-Ann's heart began that peculiar beating. "You—er—you wouldn't happen to be..."

She paused. If he was the meanie, she didn't want to know. Not tonight. Besides, he probably owned only the unit he lived in. The meanie had complained for the entire building.

Kelly-Ann became very quiet as she studied the expensive-looking condominium highlighted by outside lights. It was very beautiful, but much too sculpted and stark for her tastes.

Steve stopped the car. He'd suspected Kelly-Ann was going to ask if he'd been the man phoning her, complaining about her animals, and, he recalled, accusing her of being a bad neighbor. He wanted this night with her, unspoiled by any more suspicion, uncertainty and doubt.

"Here we are," he said with forced cheer.

Kelly-Ann waited until he opened her car door, then she composed herself, smiled and climbed out. She would concentrate on the positive. She was eager to meet Carlene and see Jeffy again.

A sudden bright thought struck her: surely a man who had a dog himself, or at least had gotten a dog for his sister, wouldn't be the kind of person to call her up and rave like a madman!

"Why do you take Jeffy to shop Number Two when Number One is in your area?" she asked curiously.

"One of her admirers told me about Suzette," he answered candidly. "I wanted to take Jeffy to someone somebody knew, and I didn't know where to start. I think this guy has a crush on her."

Kelly-Ann smiled. "Him and half of Martinsville."

"Steve? Steve?" a cultured young voice called out.

"Coming, Carlene," he replied, ushering Kelly-Ann into the kitchen through the door to the garage.

She glanced around, trying not to be too obvious. Jeffy might live here with Steve, but there wasn't a dog hair in sight. In fact, in the gleaming chrome and black-and-white kitchen, nothing was in sight. Not a pot, not a pan, not a plant, not a dirty glass.

A lovely young lady appeared in the doorway. "Hi," she said brightly.

Kelly-Ann noticed the family resemblance right away. Carlene had Steve's unruly hair and his dark eyes.

"I'm Carlene," the girl said, not waiting for the introductions. "Did Steve do it? Did he help at your pet shop?"

Kelly-Ann laughed. "He did it."

"Incredible!" Carlene cried. "Mr. Neat! Mr. Clean! Mr. There's-A-Place-For-Everything on his hands and knees with the dirty dogs and cats! I wish I'd seen that. It would have been terribly thrilling!"

Steve smiled wryly. "I wasn't on my hands and knees, and there were no cats to bathe, Carlene." He smiled at Kelly-Ann. "This, as you already know, is my darling sister, Carlene."

Kelly-Ann extended her hand, and Carlene moved forward to take it. Kelly-Ann felt bad when she noticed the girl's limp, and her concern was obvious.

"It's okay," Carlene announced casually before Kelly-Ann could speak. "You should have seen me with both legs broken, lying in that bed down the hall." She frowned. "It was awful. *I* was awful, as I'm sure my brother will tell you."

"That I will," Steve agreed. He reached out to ruffle her hair. "But we managed, didn't we?" he asked, winking at her. He motioned to the refrigerator. "Kitten, get Kelly-Ann something to drink while I change clothes, okay?"

"Sure," she said.

"Sit down," Steve invited, indicating a plush dinette that made Kelly-Ann's antique dining room set look pitiful in comparison. "I won't be long."

Settling uncomfortably on the high-back chair, Kelly-Ann watched while Carlene, chattering animatedly about Jeffy, got two sodas for them.

"Is this all right?" the girl asked, holding one out. She laughed. "I'm afraid all those blue-blood manners have escaped me here in my brother's condo. I *have* been awful, but I feel like a bird in a cage. Only now am I able to get about after months of lying in bed!"

"I'm so sorry such a thing happened to you," Kelly-Ann said sympathetically.

Shrugging, Carlene admitted, "I was showing off. I suppose I deserved it."

"Nobody deserves such a fate!" Kelly-Ann exclaimed.

"Especially Steve," Carlene said with a giggle. "Poor brother. He's such a stickler for routine and ritual—a trait he got from Daddy and military school, I'm sure. He didn't know what he was getting into with me when he offered me a home! He got Jeffy for me out of desperation, and look what happened!"

Although Kelly-Ann wanted to hear more about Steve's background, instinct warned her to stay with a safe subject. "Where is Jeffy?" she asked.

"He's in the small yard out back. He's had quite a day, and I wanted him to use up a little energy before we went to bed. I was beginning to wonder if Steve was ever coming home. I couldn't believe it when he told me he'd be working at your shop a few hours!"

Kelly-Ann smiled. "He got quite good at it, but thank heavens, Pierre, my assistant, is coming back to work."

"Would you let me help out some in the shop?" Carlene asked eagerly, brown eyes sparkling. "I'll be getting around well soon. I can come home from school on weekends."

Steve showed up, and Carlene became quiet. "What are you plotting, Carlene?"

She smiled vaguely. "Nothing. I'm just talking to Kelly-Ann."

Although he looked quizzical, he didn't press the girl. He was still buttoning his shirt when Carlene giggled.

"Steve, that shirt looks dreadful with those pants. You're wearing lime and turquoise."

Kelly-Ann was both amused and sympathetic when a blush crept up Steve's neck.

"Thank you for being so tactful, little sister," he said dryly. "Kelly-Ann," he called, retreating toward his bedroom, "please *discreetly* help me match a shirt with my pants."

Surprised by the request, Kelly-Ann followed him. She was taken aback by the severeness of the large room. It held all the furniture one usually expects in a bedroom, but none of the coziness. Her heart sank as she went with Steve to an extremely orderly compartmentalized closet. She had a feeling she understood how Carlene had felt when she moved in with Steve.

"These are supposed to be the blues," he said, indicating a line of short-sleeved shirts. "I don't know how this one sneaked in," he said, pointing to his lime shirt.

"It's only a little off color for your slacks," she murmured gently, all the time thinking what a difference a shade could make and how upset Steve would be if he really knew how startling his color combination was.

She pulled out a pale blue shirt and handed it to him. "Try this one." Then, mesmerized, she watched as he slipped the garment on.

"Is this one all right?" he asked.

"It's fine," she said.

"Then let's be on our way." He held up a small plastic case. "I'll put *my* unmentionable in with yours."

Kelly-Ann didn't know why the thought was disconcerting. It made sense; they would only have to carry one bag.

"Fine," she murmured.

Kelly-Ann had never gone to a private club before, and she found it a veritable island of pleasure. Men and women were gathered around a lovely lounge that featured a gardenlike atmosphere, complete with dozens of blooming plants, exquisite wrought-iron tables and chairs, several slowly turning ceiling fans and soft music.

"This is wonderful," she told Steve as he led her past the room. Laughter and chatter filtering out to the hallway induced Kelly-Ann to peer back over her shoulder.

Steve laughed deep and low. "I think you're going to enjoy this evening."

"I think so, too," she agreed. "Very much." But then, how could she not?

He led her beyond the workout room to the dressing rooms. "You can hang your dress in a locker. There's an attendant. Don't be afraid to leave your purse there.''

Anticipation swirling inside her, Kelly-Ann entered the room.

"Shall I help you undress?" the pleasant attendant asked.

Embarrassed, Kelly-Ann shook her head. She hadn't had anyone help her undress since she was a child and her mother used to put her to bed!

As she pulled the muumuu over her head, she wondered what kind of swimsuit Steve would wear. She adjusted her own while she critically scanned her reflection in the mirror. She was so nervous!

When she had taken off her glasses and put them in her purse, she went back out into the hall. She found Steve waiting for her, and, to her immense relief, he didn't leave her guessing about her appeal.

"You are lovely, Kelly-Ann Keernan," he murmured, his voice husky. "You have the most beautiful legs I've ever seen."

Kelly-Ann blushed feverishly. That was the third thing he'd told her that no one else ever had. First she was beautiful. Then her sweet voice. Now her legs.

"Thank you, Steve," she all but whispered self-consciously, studying his face for signs that he was being truthful. "Oh, I do hope you're sincere!" she blurted, then immediately turned even redder. Good grief! Why had she gone and said that?

Before she could think of any way to save herself, Steve pulled her toward him. She felt her pulse race as he held her hips to his, the hair on his stomach and chest tickling her lightly. Cupping her chin, he forced her to meet his eyes. Even without her glasses, as

myopic as she was, she could see that he meant what
he'd said.

"I have no reason to lie to you," he whispered
thickly. He couldn't imagine this charming woman
doubting her attractiveness.

"Thank you, Steve," she murmured tremulously.
She was so breathless that she could hardly think.

Steve seemed to hold her for an eternity while she
trembled in anticipation of—she didn't know what. A
kiss? More flattery? Or just his tantalizing touch?

He was studying her face from her hair to her chin,
and Kelly-Ann could only think that she knew her
mouth was quivering. She parted her lips in an attempt to breathe easier. She felt as if she was on fire.

Steve lowered his head at the unintentional invita-
tion of Kelly-Ann's parted mouth. He found her so seductive. She was a beauty in that brief bathing suit, and
he wanted her now more than he'd ever wanted another woman in his life.

Someone called Steve by name, and he and Kelly-
Ann drew apart. Both of them were breathing hard as
Steve threw up his hand in recognition of the other
man.

"Are you going into the Jacuzzi?" the interloper
asked.

"In a few minutes," Steve said, leading Kelly-Ann
farther down the hall. He told himself that he should
be grateful for the intruder, but he wasn't. He cleared
his throat and tried to concentrate on something besides the woman at his side. The club was no place to
get romantic!

"I have a treat for you, if you've never had it done,"
he murmured. "And even if you *have*, it'll be a treat."

"What?" she asked, thinking *he* was the only treat she really wanted.

"A massage."

Kelly-Ann wasn't sure that was going to be such a treat. "A massage, a real massage?" she questioned.

Steve laughed again. "I hope it's real. It sure feels like it when the masseur does it."

"A man?" Kelly-Ann all but wailed.

Steve chuckled. "For me, yes. For you, no. You have a masseuse."

"That's a relief," she said, and even at that, she was uncertain about it.

"You'll love it," he promised when they went into yet another room.

Kelly-Ann wondered.

Thirty minutes later, every muscle in her body feeling like melted butter, she met Steve in the outer room.

"How was it?" he asked, though he could tell from the serene look on her face.

"I think I died and went to heaven," she replied.

He laughed as he led her to the Jacuzzi, where she experienced an equally delightful treat. The hot, swirling water soothed her muscles even more, but the most delightful part of the Jacuzzi was Steve there by her side, relaxing in silence with her and near enough to touch.

"Let's take a quick shower and go eat," he said after about ten minutes. "I'm hungry."

Kelly-Ann had forgotten all about dinner. She had her eyes closed, and her head was resting on the edge of the tub. "This is much too wonderful to leave," she said dreamily.

He smiled. "The hot water soon becomes too draining. It's called 'too much of a good thing.' We really should get out. We can come again whenever you like."

Her eyes opening instantly, Kelly-Ann tried to focus on Steve's face. He wanted to see her again after tonight! He had just told her a few minutes ago that he had no reason to lie. He wasn't disillusioned with her or her house or pets. He *couldn't* be the meanie who called her from the condos.

Kelly-Ann's heart took flight. She found it most appropriate that Steve should indicate he cared, there in the warm, caressing water. After all, they were water signs.

Steve met her excited green eyes and saw emotions he wasn't ready to see. Hell! He would have to be more careful about what he said. He was feverishly trying to think of ways to lessen the impact of his statement, to put some distance between him and this woman. Why had he said they could come anytime?

He drew in a steadying breath. He'd said it because he liked Kelly-Ann, because she'd found pleasure here at the club and because he was pleased he'd brought her. He'd said it, he reasoned, because they *could* come anytime.

That didn't mean he'd made any kind of future commitment to the woman. He could bring her as a guest whenever she liked. She could even come alone with his say-so at the front desk. *He* didn't have to come at all for her to use the facilities.

"Ready?" he asked, standing up suddenly.

Kelly-Ann wasn't ready, but she knew he was. Right before her eyes, he had changed again! She didn't know what had happened; she heard the coolness in his voice. She saw it in his stance. And this time he didn't hold out his hand for hers.

She felt that sinking feeling again. Pisces man: warm one moment; cold the next.

She truly didn't think she could stand someone that wishy-washy in her life. Steve Jamison constantly caught her in heaven or hell, and both extremes were too much for her to handle.

Chapter Eleven

Once they were in the car, silence descended again. Kelly-Ann looked at Steve, but he didn't look back. Lost in his thoughts, he was gripping the steering wheel tightly.

She sighed. Her appetite had disappeared completely. It really was late; now she wanted to climb in her bed and forget this extraordinary day. Too much had happened too quickly.

"I'm not hungry now," she announced, trying to sound nonchalant. "If I eat this late, I'll be awake all night, and I do have to get up and finish bathing the rest of the animals so they can go home, too. You don't mind if I skip dinner tonight, do you?"

Steve glanced at her, surprised. He realized he didn't want to eat, either, yet he'd insisted on dinner and felt that he couldn't beg off.

Forcing himself to smile, he said, "Well, if you're *that* tired, I suppose I can let you off the hook."

He didn't know quite what to think when she looked terribly downcast. It was very late, and she'd said she didn't want to eat. So had he, to himself, but now, watching Kelly-Ann, he felt like eating everything on the menu just to ease his frustration and guilt over his indecision.

No, he told himself, it wasn't really indecision. He was getting in too deep too soon with this woman. They needed some breathing space. Subconsciously, he thought they both knew it was literally time to call it a night.

"I'll let you off the hook," he continued, as if minutes hadn't lapsed, "if you'll go to dinner with me Sunday night."

Wishing she could keep the relief out of her voice, Kelly-Ann murmured, "I guess I could do that. After all, I did agree to dinner, didn't I?"

She didn't want to deal with how upset she'd been at his quick capitulation on the meal tonight—and worse, she'd been afraid he wasn't going to ask her out again.

"Yes, you did," he said. "I'll pick you up at seven."

"Fine," she agreed.

Once again, she wondered what was fine. She wasn't. She didn't think Steve was, either.

And, still, as much as she wanted to go home right now, she couldn't wait to see him again!

Two long days passed before Sunday evening finally arrived. Kelly-Ann was dressed and waiting by six-thirty. She hated her eagerness, but she couldn't help herself. She'd pored over her daily horoscope, interpreting the prediction of an exciting and productive day all kinds of ways. So far, the day had been neither.

When the doorbell rang, her dogs started barking and she jumped. Smoothing down her full-skirted forest-green dress, she rushed to open the door. Steve was standing there in a three-piece brown suit, looking splendid.

"You look lovely," he told her, interrupting her thoughts.

"You, too," she said, smiling warmly. "I mean you look handsome."

Both of them laughed, and Kelly-Ann cautioned herself to watch what her silly tongue said. More than anything in the entire world, she wanted this night to be magical.

Well, maybe that wasn't what she wanted more than anything in the world, she amended, as Steve took her hand and walked with her to his car. More than anything, she was afraid she wanted him. And that was scary.

The Mexican restaurant he chose was authentic, she soon found, and, at once, she was given something else to focus on besides Steve. Even though she'd said she liked her food spicy, she gasped when she sampled a chip covered with tempting salsa.

"It's so hot!" she cried.

"Very hot," he agreed. "The peppers are supposed to be good for you, believe it or not. That fact aside, they're delicious."

She began to fan her mouth with her hand, as if that would do any good. "My mouth is on fire!" she exclaimed.

"Oh, you don't like the salsa?" Steve asked, frowning. "I'm sorry. I thought you wanted it hot."

Kelly-Ann tried to laugh, but her eyes were watering and she feared tears would run down her face. "I said I liked it hot, not on fire!" she protested.

He held out a plain tortilla chip to her. "Any kind of bread is supposed to take away some of the fire, though I'm afraid once your taste buds are seared, nothing will ease the burning, not even water. I'll order a milder salsa for you."

Suspecting that he was disappointed, she shook her head. "No, I like this. I really do, and now that I'm seared, it won't matter, will it?"

He grinned. "No, I suppose not, except that you really shouldn't eat more if you *don't* like it."

"I do," she said firmly, taking another bite, much smaller, to prove her point. She wanted to like the salsa spicy because he liked it that way.

Unexpectedly, Steve slid back his chair and came over to the bench across the table where Kelly-Ann was sitting. He eased in beside her, tilted her chin and lightly brushed her mouth with his.

"There," he said gently, "does that feel better?"

That was all it took for Kelly-Ann to forget the way Steve had unsettled her when he left the Jacuzzi so suddenly two days ago. What she remembered now was how he'd kissed her wrist at lunch time, sending crazy sensations spinning through her.

Her stomach started somersaulting. She was dying for this man to give her a real kiss, a passionate kiss, the kiss she'd been expecting when he helped her at the shop. He came closer and closer each time, yet he didn't quite manage to touch her mouth as she longed for him to do.

When the waiter came to take their order, Kelly-Ann mumbled distractedly; she could no longer concentrate on food. She didn't care what she ordered or how hot anything was or wasn't. Nothing could be as flaming hot as she was with Steve Jamison seated right next to her.

When they had finished the meal with an ice-cream confection, Kelly-Ann picked up the check. "I'll get this," she said. "I didn't pay you for helping me."

"No way," Steve said. "I enjoyed it."

"Really, I insist," she said. "Either that, or accept money for the hours you worked."

He reached across and chucked her chin. "Stubborn and passionate and beautiful all in one. You're quite a package, Miss Keernan."

Afraid that her body was going to start reacting to his touch, she fumbled in her purse for money to pay the check.

Steve smoothly pulled out a single large bill and put it on the tray. "If you must repay me, I'll take that kiss you lost when you bet I couldn't bathe Sadie," he said.

Her emerald eyes grew large. "Here?" she asked.

He laughed. "Not here. Later. Are you ready, Kelly-Ann?"

She was ready! Flushed and fluttery, she hurried with him from the restaurant. She had been so eager for his kiss that she would have accepted it in the restaurant!

"You didn't particularly enjoy the food, did you?" Steve asked, startling her out of her introspection.

"Oh, I did," she insisted.

"You only played with it," he noted. "I thought you weren't satisfied."

She looked at him in surprise. If she'd played with her food, it had been because he was by her side, distracting her from anything but him. She felt that she was well fed.

But satisfied? She doubted it. She didn't think anything could satisfy her except Steve.

All the way back to her house, she sat in tense expectation of how the evening would finally end. She tried to relax, but she knew she was anticipating Steve's kiss.

The ride home seemed incredibly long, though they finally got there. In a stupor, Kelly-Ann walked with Steve toward her front door.

"Good night, pretty woman," he said, his brown eyes searching her upturned face.

Steve seemed to be stuck to the sidewalk leading to her porch. In his mind, he knew that he had done all the right things to help her enjoy the evening. Now it was over. His mind told him to forget the kiss he'd talked about and go home, but his body had other ideas. He had been waiting for this very moment, he realized, since he went into the club with her two nights ago.

He'd ached to kiss her there in the hall. No, he admitted, he'd wanted to kiss her earlier than that. He'd wanted to kiss her when he'd first looked at that cupid's-bow mouth in the shop, and again when he'd taken her to lunch, and again...

Countless times, he confessed to himself, he'd wanted to kiss this woman. He didn't intend to wait any longer. Drawing her into his arms, he lowered his head and at last, he sampled those enticing red lips. They were sweet, incredibly, deliciously sweet.

Kelly-Ann emitted a soft sigh of satisfaction as Steve caressed her mouth with his. She relished the skill of his lips as they coaxed hers into total response, tantalizing and teasing, caressing lightly, then pressing more urgently, seeking all she would give.

And she had so very much to give. She had wanted to be loved by this man all day! And now she didn't want to miss an intoxicating moment of his sexiness, his sensuality, his loving.

She quickly discovered she wasn't prepared in the least for Steve Jamison's loving. She was traveling through time at breakneck speed as he led her deeper into a terribly exciting, very unfamiliar vortex of sensual delight.

Her satisfaction slipped into hunger, then sped into burning passion as Steve savored her kiss, his tongue meeting hers in an ancient, meaningful ritual of desire. She opened her parted lips more fully so that she might indulge the seductive mating of their tongues, the enticing lure of his as it entered her mouth, stroked her tongue, then retreated.

When he drew her bottom lip between his lips to tease it, Kelly-Ann felt warm all over.

Wrapping her arms around Steve, she pulled him tighter against her body, wanting him to somehow stop the ache that throbbed deep inside her, wanting him to suppress the need, to satisfy her urgent hunger.

Steve thought he had wanted to kiss this woman, but he hadn't been prepared for the depth of desire she was obviously capable of.

No, he told himself, trying to reason at a time past all reason, he had suspected Kelly-Ann was capable of deep passion, for she had shown how passionate she was in everything, from dealing with the animals to indulging in the pampering offered at his private club. Nevertheless, this creature in his arms, this warm, open, willing woman, was more than he had bargained for. Much more.

His heart was pounding, his pulse was racing, his mouth began to say things he wouldn't allow his brain to even think.

"You feel so wonderful," he heard himself murmuring. "You taste wonderful. You're incredibly loving."

Then he lost his train of thought as Kelly-Ann held him against her shapely body as if she never wanted to let him go. He didn't want her to. He wanted this night to go on forever, to feel her in his arms, to caress her mouth with his and feel her feverish response, he wanted to—

Damn! What was he doing? What was he thinking? Or *not* thinking?

He untangled her arms from his and stepped back while he still could, before he said or did something as he'd done at the club, telling her she could go there anytime. He wasn't ready for all this. His brain was overworked, his imagination was running without restraints, and that didn't even begin to explain what was happening inside his body.

"Kelly-Ann," he murmured, still holding on to her hands, needing to keep them where they were, lest she draw him to her again, "I think we'd better call it a night."

Through the drifting clouds in her mind portraying the image of herself sharing eternity with this man, Kelly-Ann's brain sounded the alarm.

She opened her eyes and tried to focus. But all she saw was Steve, and that was what she wanted to see. He was still there, the handsome prince, the man she would have father her babies, live by her side, love her for eternity.

"Yes?" she whispered, pulling free of his hands as if he weren't trying to restrain her at all. She didn't know why on earth he'd stepped away. She wanted to feel him against her again, know his power and potency, have him hold her so hard that the ache inside her would be crushed, or have him take her so that the desire would be sated.

"Kelly-Ann," he tried again, struggling not to get lost in her warmth as she wrapped her arms around him and held on tightly. "It's been a nice evening," he said, his voice hoarse, his breathing labored.

"Yes, it has," she said in that sweet, sweet voice, "a wonderful one, Steve." She looked up into his eyes. "Thank you," she whispered. "Thank you very much for—for everything—not staying mad about Jeffy, taking me to lunch, helping me at the shop, and..."

Her words trailed away as she giggled sweetly. "And..." She wanted to say *and for loving me,* but she didn't dare. "And taking me to dinner," she finally gasped out.

Steve felt as though he were burning up inside, both from fever and fear. Yes, it had been wonderful, and yes, he had done all those things—and more. Much more.

What was he doing? This woman was the loony pet groomer with a house full of animals, and he was the computer-software creator who lived just across the way. The fence that separated them divided their lives as well as their life-styles.

"Steve," she murmured sweetly, "kiss me again."

Oh, Lord in heaven, he told himself, didn't the woman know he was trying to *stop* kissing her? Wasn't she listening? And if she was, had she heard?

He tried to keep his mind on leaving when he looked down into her face. Those green eyes were sparkling like emeralds in the scant light. Her lips had been kissed already until they were full and pouting. Her dimples were showing as she smiled up at him.

He resisted. He resisted with all his might, but how could he refuse her one more kiss? What could he say without hurting her feelings? Out of the mainstream of reality though she was, she was also much too adorable to hurt.

He bent his head again and touched her lips, meaning to give her only a tiny kiss, a stingy kiss that he could take back if he wanted to. But that was impossible.

Kelly-Ann Keernan parted those pretty cupid's-bow lips, molded them against his and caressed his mouth in the most incredibly provocative way. Her tongue found his, and the flames that ignited in Steve almost burned him up before he could draw away a second time.

He was sure his arm was shaking when he deliberately looked down at his watch, even though he couldn't have seen it with a flashlight.

"It's late," he said thickly, almost rasping. Didn't this woman know she *had* to go in?

"Steve?" she asked questioningly.

He was turning cold on her again. She hadn't thought it possible. Not after they'd kissed like this, held each other this way. Why, she was still in his arms!

She looked up into his eyes, but it was too late. She'd lost him. A tiny whimper of regret escaped her lips. She didn't understand Steve Jamison. She believed in her heart that he was sincere, that he cared for her, but in her head, she didn't know what to think.

"Good night, Kelly-Ann," he said gently, his voice almost breaking. Lord in heaven, he didn't know what was wrong with him. He didn't want to walk away from her; yet he knew he shouldn't stay.

Kelly-Ann licked her lips, which had suddenly gone from moist and warm to dry and parched. She hunted for the two words, two simple words that would end this night with a little dignity and courtesy.

But she couldn't find them.

What had Steve said? *Good night*. That's what *he'd* said. Those were the words she was looking for, yet they were not the words she wanted. They were so…so inconclusive.

Good wasn't the right word at all for the bad feeling she suddenly had inside. *Night* was a little better, for it meant the end of the day, and only the stars knew what else. And it could allude to any number of dark feelings she was beginning to experience.

"Good night," she parroted.

And then, like the silly dreamer she was, she waited, for surely there must be more. Wasn't he going to say he would call her? He would see her at the shop?

Steve Jamison turned toward his car without looking back. Kelly-Ann had the feeling that the bottom
had just dropped out of the box that held her dreams.
They were falling to the sidewalk with each step this
man took, and she didn't know how to catch them,
how to hold on to them.

With shaking hands, she found her house key and
rushed into the sanctity of her home. Her pets eagerly
came to see her, and somehow, she smiled at them
through her tears.

One week went by. Then another. Kelly-Ann had
caught up with her work and the shops fell back into
their regular routine, with Pierre helping at Number
One in the morning and Number Two in the afternoon.

People came and went, as before, with the usual dogs
and cats and occasional other less ordinary animals
needing to be groomed. Their owners greeted Kelly-
Ann and smiled, and she smiled in return. Life returned to normal, to the way it had always been, with
the exception of those two extraordinary days Steve
had shared with her.

And with the exception that all day long, Kelly-Ann
waited for the phone to ring at work. When she was
home, she waited for it to ring there. She even called
Suzette and asked if Steve Jamison had brought Jeffy
back in to be groomed, because, of course, he'd missed
his grooming day.

But there was no word from Steve or about Steve.
Kelly-Ann constantly whispered to her heart, telling it
to hush, to stop asking questions and wondering and

worrying about what had gone wrong. She and Steve had matched only with their sun signs.

Or rather, Steve had matched her sun sign and nothing more. She thought she matched everything about him, from the way he kissed to the way he laughed.

She shook her head. That wasn't true and she knew it.

Sure, she'd gone like a fool and fallen head-over-heels in love at first sight—even if it had taken forty-eight hours, and even if she'd known when they argued during the first five minutes they met, that they weren't suited.

Her brain told her that. Her brain had told her all along how ridiculous she was being. But her brain didn't think for her heart, only her head. It didn't know how to tell her heart to stop hurting.

Steve threw himself back into his work with pretended gusto. He'd taken enough time off to see Carlene through the major part of her crisis. Now, thanks to circumstances, Carlene was absorbed in her own interests, poring over catalogs, trying to decide how much education was required for various animal-related careers, like veterinarian or animal-behavior therapist.

Nina Bromberg, the talent scout, had called from California to discuss Jeffy's commercial career, and though Carlene was excited, she seemed too engrossed in her future plans to focus solely on Jeffy and his commercial prospects.

She was planning to handle him herself at the next dog show, but even that had paled in the face of her ardent search for a career.

Teenagers, Steve thought, off on one tangent one day, on another the next. He supposed it was all part of growing up, part of finding one's place in the scheme of things.

He'd done the same thing when he was young, daydreaming about the future, making plans. There had been a battle, he recalled, between him and his father, a clash of wills about what he considered an interesting career and his father's plans for him to pursue a military career. But he didn't want to think about that. He looked out the window of the tall building where he worked.

Ironically, he was daydreaming more now than he ever had, his mind drifting off at the sound of a dog on the street, the sight of a cat, the song of a bird. And those were just his daydreams. His night dreams were full of Kelly-Ann Keernan, no matter how firmly he told himself not to dream of her.

They could never work out as a couple! How on earth could he live with her and that menagerie?

Sure, he'd grown very attached to Jeffy. That was different. Jeffy fit into a category, a place in Steve's daily life. He knew what to expect from Jeffy, and Jeffy knew what to expect from him. That wasn't the same as taking in stray animals of every description, working one's entire existence around dogs and cats and parrots and parakeets. The mess, the noise, the craziness. That was her life.

Oh, but how he'd loved Kelly-Ann's sweetness, her concern for her creatures, her passion. He'd spent two days out of his life with her. And two weeks without her. He'd missed her terribly the first week; if possible, the second one was even worse.

There was no denying it. He'd wanted to see her badly. He'd even driven by the shop twice; at home, he'd gotten out of his car at the curb of the condos and looked over the fence at that sprawling old house of hers. In the daylight . . .

This had to stop! He reached for the phone and dialed a number.

"Janet," he said when the woman answered, "are you free this evening? Would you like to have dinner?"

When he received a positive reply, he told Janet what time he would pick her up, then replaced the receiver.

"There," he said aloud. "That will give you someone else to think about." A picture of Janet, with her sophisticated look, short, sleek blond hair and her tall model's figure filled his mind.

The image was soon completely overtaken by a sexy, fuller-figured woman with pretty legs and long wavy hair.

"Hell!" Steve muttered, shoving back his chair.

There was no use staying here. He couldn't get any work done. But then, he'd been saying that every day this week!

Chapter Twelve

Kelly-Ann was surprised when the call came from Carlene. She'd known the teenager was interested in working in the shop, and she'd fully intended to talk to the girl. But she'd felt too uncomfortable after Steve made no effort to see her again. She didn't want him to think that she was chasing him.

"Hi, Carlene," she said. "How are you? How's Jeffy?" *And how's Steve?* she really wanted to ask.

"I'm doing great, Kelly-Ann," the teenager said. "I just wondered what happened to you. I asked Steve...well, anyway, I'm still hoping you'll let me work in your shop. I was trying to talk to you about it the night he took you out to dinner...."

Kelly-Ann didn't tell Carlene they didn't go to dinner that night. In fact, she didn't know what to say to Steve's sister.

There was another awkward pause. "Anyway," Carlene continued, "I wondered if I could see the shop, or we could talk or something. I'm really interested in animals and I want to ask you absolutely everything."

Kelly-Ann heard a cracking sound somewhere in the vicinity of her heart. Did the girl know what she was doing? Kelly-Ann shook her head. Of course not. Carlene was interested in animals and Kelly-Ann was someone who had information.

Carlene obviously knew that Steve wasn't interested in Kelly-Ann but she couldn't know how much Kelly-Ann cared for him. She felt another pain strike her heart.

For two long, agonizing weeks, she had clung to the dream that Steve would call her, that he cared for her as she did for him, that Cupid was on her side.

Steve hadn't called. And now she knew he wouldn't.

Kelly-Ann liked Carlene, and she'd wanted to be friendly with the girl. She would simply have to put her emotions aside and get on with life. It would be easy. Very easy. Like dropping off the end of the earth.

"I'd be delighted to talk to you," she heard herself saying distantly. "How about dinner tonight? I'm free if you are."

There was no point in adding that she was free every night now. She decided that she needed some company as badly as Carlene. She just didn't know how she could be around this girl, who looked so much like her brother, and not be torn apart.

"Great!" Carlene cried. "I really appreciate it, Kelly-Ann. Listen, I can meet you someplace if you like, or I can come to your place. I'm driving again now. My leg's doing fine and anyway, the reinjured one is the left, so it doesn't affect my driving.''

Kelly-Ann smiled as she listened to the animated teenager. She would have to do her best not to be melancholy tonight. Carlene needed some variety in her life, and, Kelly-Ann told herself, so did she.

"I just live right across the fence from you," she said. "In the big old house with the animals—"

"You're kidding!" Carlene cried. "You're the loon—"

Kelly-Ann bit down on her lip. Then she finished the sentence for the girl. "The loony woman with all those annoying animals. The one your brother called several times."

"I never complained about the noise," Carlene said quickly. "I mean, after all, most of the people here throw parties and stuff. And myself, I figure live and let live. Sometimes I'd walk to the fence to try to figure out what was making that screeching noise every morning."

The teenager laughed nervously. "Kelly-Ann, you're not mad at *me* for those calls, are you? Steve made them because two other people in the building insisted. Steve owns the building."

Kelly-Ann felt her eyes fill with tears. "Of course, I'm not mad at you," she said, trying to control her quavering voice. "In fact, why don't you drive over to the house and I'll show you what's making the noise. I'm on my way home from work now. It'll only take me a minute. See you there."

She replaced the phone without giving Carlene a chance to confirm or deny the plans. She couldn't say anything else if she had to.

No wonder Steve hadn't called her again. She'd been right. He *was* the meanie who'd raged at her about the castaways and the regulars at her house, the forgotten and unwanted animals he saw as a nuisance.

And no wonder she loved those poor creatures. At this moment, she felt exactly like one. Now she knew that Steve Jamison could never love her.

Kelly-Ann had forced herself into a more positive frame of mind by the time she reached her house. She wasn't surprised to see a sunny-yellow compact car parked in the drive. She had no doubt that it was Carlene's, and the girl quickly appeared to confirm her belief.

"Hi, Kelly-Ann!" the sixteen-year-old cried exuberantly. "Your place is so wild! Jeffy would love to be turned loose here!"

Smiling at the girl's enthusiasm, Kelly-Ann nodded. "Yes, I suspect he would. My animals love it."

"I saw a rabbit around back," Carlene said. Then she blushed. "I hope you didn't mind my going around there. I just had to check out everything! I couldn't wait for you. This place is so crazy—I mean wild—I—"

Kelly-Ann put her arm around Carlene's shoulders. "I know what you mean, and it's fine. The place is crazy and wild and bizarre and all of that. It's also home for me and my animal friends. Come on in and meet them."

"It really is neat," Carlene said, searching for a compliment that suited. "I don't mean in the usual sense of the word," she hurried to say. "Oh, Kelly-Ann!" she wailed, realizing how she sounded. "I'm making an absolute dummy of myself and hurting your feelings, when really I'm trying to say I like your house and pets.''

Kelly-Ann squeezed Carlene's shoulders. "Relax, Carlene. There's no reason in the world to get yourself in a dither because you're uncomfortable about Steve and me. I like you, and I know you'll like my home. Come on inside and let me introduce you to the occupants.''

She was sincere. She knew Carlene, unlike Steve, wouldn't be ill at ease with the clutter of creatures and things. "What's your sign?" she asked suddenly.

Carlene smiled. "Pisces, the same as Steve's. Isn't that something? We were almost born on the same day, but I trailed behind by twenty-nine hours and fourteen years.''

Thank God for small favors, Kelly-Ann told herself. She'd almost begun to doubt the wisdom of her earlier words. Not another Pisces! She couldn't cope!

"We celebrate our birthdays on the same day," Carlene said proudly. "Though not together," she added less energetically. "He's usually here, and I'm usually away at boarding school in northern Virginia.''

"Oh," Kelly-Ann said, looking back over her shoulder at the tall teenager. "You miss your family, don't you?"

Carlene looked embarrassed and shrugged. "I've *always* been away at school," she said. "Steve, too, though he must not have minded.''

"Really?" Kelly-Ann asked, opening the door. "I thought you didn't mind. I understood that you wanted to stay here in Martinsville with Steve because you loved your school.''

Carlene's big brown eyes met Kelly-Ann's briefly. "Our parents shouldn't have had children," she said, her young voice judgmental. "Mother and Father only need each other. I think Steve and I are nuisances to them."

"No!" Kelly-Ann protested. "You're wrong, Carlene."

The young girl shook her head. "You don't know my family, Kelly-Ann. I wasn't planned."

She laughed bitterly. "In fact, I was such a total surprise, Mother and Father delayed a move because of me. That's the truth. Father won a prize position as a foreign diplomat when he retired from the service. He and Mother thought they were all through with children when they had Steve."

She shrugged with a carelessness that Kelly-Ann knew was pretend. "Then I turned up to mess up their plans." She looked away. "But it doesn't matter. I'm almost grown now."

Her face grew expressive again. "That's why I wanted so much to talk to you. I see your appearance in my life as fate, Kelly-Ann. I know you're going to think this is crazy, but I believe in predestination. I've been going nuts trying to decide what to do with my life, and all my parents have done is harp on the necessity to decide upon a career."

Kelly-Ann interrupted her to coax her inside. "Come on. Sit down," she managed to interject.

"If I don't decide soon," Carlene continued, barely watching what she was doing as she waded through the animals greeting Kelly-Ann warmly, "they'll decide for me. I know they will."

"You're young, and things seem worse than they are," Kelly-Ann assured Carlene, all her typical Cancer sun-sign maternal instincts working overtime. She found herself thinking that the poor thing was as helpless as a stray animal. If her parents were really as she said, and Kelly-Ann knew that teenage girls tended to overdramatize, she felt sorry for her.

Carlene shook her head. "My father says he didn't pour all his money into my education to have me daydream my life away, or to marry some man and waste my brains cleaning up houses and messy children."

"Great Scot!" Kelly-Ann blurted. "Surely the man knows you have a right to make your own decisions about your life. Why, I myself, want..."

She let her words trail off. She didn't need to tell Steve's sister that she wanted seven children, either. In fact, although she cared for the girl already and wanted to be totally honest and uninhibited with her, Kelly-Ann knew that most of what she said would get back to Steve. And she didn't want that man knowing any more about her than he already did.

"It's your life, it's your life, take it easy, take it easy," the parrot suddenly squawked, causing Carlene to rush over to the cage.

"He talks!" she exclaimed.

"Yes, indeed he does," Kelly-Ann couldn't help but say dryly. "He's one of the reasons for the complaints in your condo, I suspect. But only one. Here," she said, "let me introduce you to the other creatures who live with me."

Half an hour later, Carlene was still euphoric about Kelly-Ann, her regular animals and her charity cases.

Her mind spinning, her chatter coming a mile a minute, Carlene began to talk about how she'd always wanted pets and how she'd never been allowed any until she moved in with Steve. It was destiny, she proclaimed, for once she got Jeffy, she knew she wanted to spend her life working with animals.

"You will let me help out at the shop, won't you?" she interrupted herself to plead.

Kelly-Ann smiled. How could she refuse? She didn't usually work on Saturdays, but she had many customers who had asked her about weekends. They would be more apt to leave their animals when they weren't so busy with the work week, they'd told her, and she knew that would also allow them to do chores without their pets underfoot.

"Let's go eat and we'll talk about it," Kelly-Ann said. "I believe we can work something out."

"I know a great little Italian restaurant Steve takes me to," Carlene cried. "If you like Italian food, you'll be nuts about this."

Kelly-Ann nodded, the memory of the restaurant Carlene must be talking about still too fresh in her mind. "I don't think I'm in the mood for Italian tonight. How—"

"I know a great Mexican place, then," Carlene interrupted. "It has something for everyone. Let's go there."

"All right," Kelly-Ann said with resignation. After all, there were only so many places to eat in town; there was no point in debating the issue further.

* * *

A short time later, they walked into the Mexican restaurant. They had just started toward a table when Carlene spotted Steve.

"There's my brother!" she sang out, leaving Kelly-Ann no decent route of escape without looking as though she was running away.

Which she did, indeed, want to do. Steve Jamison was sitting with an exquisite blond woman who was clearly enamored of him. Kelly-Ann was sure she couldn't eat a thing; her stomach had started that hated lurching, her pulse was racing, her heart was pounding.

And worse, tears were filling her eyes. Stars above, why hadn't she agreed to the Italian restaurant?

Hearing his sister, Steve stood up. "Carlene!" he said. "What a surprise. I didn't know you were going out to dinner."

Kelly-Ann was lagging behind, wishing more than anything in the world that this wasn't happening. She tried not to stare at the sleek blonde with Steve, but her gaze kept wandering to the woman. Each time she saw how exquisite she was. And each time she told herself this was the kind of woman Steve Jamison would be attracted to.

"Kelly-Ann," he murmured, drawing her attention back to him.

She didn't want to look at him, but could not avoid it. Forcing an artificial smile, she said, "Good evening, Steve."

Her voice was formal and brittle, the words clipped, and she told herself that Steve wouldn't be thinking how sweet she sounded tonight. But then, she didn't feel sweet. She felt bitter and neglected. She felt like one of her pitiful animals who hadn't lived up to the master's expectations.

"Come and join us," Steve said, his gaze still on Kelly-Ann.

"Great," Carlene said. "You look like you haven't started yet anyway."

"We were just getting ready to order," Steve said. He turned to his companion. "You don't mind, do you, Janet?"

Kelly-Ann thought that Janet looked like she'd rather break rocks on a prison farm than have them as guests for dinner, but she was gracious enough to murmur, "No, of course not."

After all, Kelly-Ann told herself, what else could the beauty say? This was her date's sister, and Kelly-Ann was— What category *did* she fall into? She didn't want to hazard a guess.

Even as she thought it, Steve was making the introductions. "Janet, this is Kelly-Ann Keernan, and, of course, my sister, Carlene. Janet Roster."

Well, Kelly-Ann thought, he did that smoothly. She didn't fall into any category. Her only saving grace was that Janet hadn't, either.

Finally a flicker of reasoning penetrated her gray matter. Her numbed mind began to work.

"We really don't want to intrude," she said, sounding much sweeter than she had before. "We'll just take a table over there."

She turned away quickly, not even knowing if there was a table available, but she wasn't quick enough.

"Nonsense," Steve said, sounding very familiar. "Join us. We'd love for you to."

Meeting his eyes again, Kelly-Ann was about to issue her second protest. She, too, had rather work on a prison farm busting rocks than sit with Steve Jamison and his date. Or, truthfully, she'd rather run home and cry. That's what she really wanted to do. She was sure she couldn't carry on idle chatter with these people.

He pulled out a chair for her, and she saw that Carlene had already sat down. Kelly-Ann looked at the girl hopefully.

"Don't you think we'd all be more comfortable, Carlene, if you and I spend our evening at another table? We want to discuss animals, and I doubt seriously if Janet and Steve want to hear all about the animal world."

"Sure we do," Steve announced, ushering Kelly-Ann into the chair.

She tried to calm down, but it wasn't possible. Her whole body was in rebellion. *She* didn't want to discuss anything with Steve Jamison and his too-too-pretty woman!

"Let's stay here, Kelly-Ann," Carlene said. "You don't mind, do you? I mean, Steve's my brother and I don't get to spend a lot of time with him." The teenager turned to Janet. "How are you this evening, Janet?"

Icy-blue eyes met sparkling brown. "In all honesty," the woman said tightly, "I've developed a splitting headache, so it's nice that you two—" she gave Kelly-Ann a brief glance "—can join your brother." She glared at Steve. "If you'll just take me home, you can enjoy your meal with your sister and her friend."

"I'm sorry to hear you're not feeling well," Steve said, trying to behave decently, even though news of her headache was the best thing he'd heard since he picked her up. In the ten minutes it had taken them to get from her beautiful home to the restaurant, he'd been bored beyond belief hearing about the stocks and bonds her aunt had left her.

Oddly enough, for he took a keen interest in the market, he'd found himself thinking that he didn't care a rat's toenail about Janet's stock and bonds. Then his mind had begun to wander, taking a seemingly natural course from rat's toenail to bunny's fur, to cats, to dogs and much too swiftly, directly to Kelly-Ann Keernan.

He'd felt guilty, it was true, though obviously not guilty enough. He'd known right from the start that dinner with Janet was a diversionary tactic, a way to try to circumvent his relentless thoughts of Kelly-Ann. Clearly the maneuver hadn't worked.

He'd never been so happy to see anyone in his life! Sweet-voiced, long-haired, dimpled-darling Kelly-Ann. She was a sight for sore eyes. He'd wanted to see her for two long, long weeks. And here she was, like a dream come true.

When Janet stood up, Steve realized that he was being inexcusably rude. He had asked the woman out, and he owed it to her and himself not to be so eager to be rid of her.

"Won't you stay?" he asked softly. "Perhaps if you ate something, you'd feel better."

"I would feel better if you took me home this instant," she said, no longer trying to act graciously.

Kelly-Ann couldn't hold back a small smile. Mr. Steve Jamison was in for more tongue-lashing if she were any judge of people. And she was glad, she told herself. It served him right.

"Excuse us," he said simply, then guided Janet toward the door.

Carlene stared after them curiously. "Well, I'll be darned," she said, "we ran the woman off, Kelly-Ann."

Kelly-Ann smiled slightly. "I'm afraid we did. But don't feel too badly. I believe it was my company she didn't like."

Carlene giggled. "Sorry! You can't take the credit. Last month I overheard her asking Steve when he was going to 'get rid of the brat.' That's *me!*" she said cheerfully.

"Carlene!" Kelly-Ann cried. "You're not serious."

"I'm as serious as a heart attack," the girl answered. "So I'm glad I gave her a headache."

Kelly-Ann frowned as a new thought occurred to her. "Did you know where they were going to eat, Carlene?"

She giggled again. "Yep. Or at least, I knew it would be one of the two restaurants I suggested to you. Steve always tells me where he's going to be in case I need him."

Kelly-Ann nodded knowingly. "And if he wasn't at the one we decided on?"

"I would have found an excuse to go to the other one," Carlene responded without hesitation.

"Oh, I do hope you're not trying to play Cupid," Kelly-Ann said earnestly. "It won't do a bit of good, I promise you."

Carlene laughed. "Little do you know, Kelly-Ann! I live with my brother. I know misery when I see it, and that man's been miserable, believe me!"

Kelly-Ann's heart began to beat erratically. She couldn't stand to hope for something that just wasn't going to happen. She was beginning to regret coming to dinner with Carlene.

"Really," she murmured, "any misery your brother feels has nothing to do with me. Unless," she added quickly, "the people in his condo building are still complaining about my animals."

"They wouldn't dare," Carlene said with youthful logic. "They don't have the nerve to complain to a man who has a dog of his own, or at least one living with him. Steve's very loyal. You saw what happened to Janet."

"Yes," Kelly-Ann said wryly. "She got invited to dinner."

Carlene laughed. "And she's being taken home because she didn't want us to join them."

"*You,*" Kelly-Ann emphasized.

"The fact is," Carlene said, "that Steve didn't really want to be with her. He wants to be with you, yet something is bugging him. I don't know what, but I do know he wants you."

Kelly-Ann shook her head, and Carlene held up her hand. "Trust me on this. I've been living with him for several months now, and let me tell you, he's been brooding, and his disposition has been awful these past two weeks. It doesn't take a genius to figure this one out. Did you see his eyes light up when he saw us?"

"No," Kelly-Ann said. She'd been too busy panicking.

"Well, you'll see," Carlene insisted, as if it were an established fact. "Steve will be back shortly. *You're* the one he really wants to be with."

Suddenly the girl blushed. "Oh, no!" she exclaimed. "That's not the problem, is it?"

"What?" Kelly-Ann cried, totally confused.

"You *are* interested in my brother, aren't you? You didn't tell him to drop dead, did you?"

Kelly-Ann laughed out loud at the unexpected question. "I'll be absolutely open with you, Carlene, since I believe that's what you're being with me. I'm *crazy* about your brother. You have no idea how crazy, but he doesn't care about me. Even though he said he did, or at least he indicated that . . . or . . ."

She threw her hands up. "Oh, I don't know what I'm saying. I thought we were getting along fine. Sure, there were problems with Jeffy, but we spent several hours together that first day. Then I went out with him on the following Sunday. I thought . . . I felt like I . . ."

Carlene nodded knowingly. "You're in love with him, aren't you?"

Beet red, Kelly-Ann agreed. "I know this sounds incredibly crazy, but I think I fell in love with Steve the first time I saw him. Oh, Carlene," she cried, realizing what she'd confessed, "you must promise not to ever repeat that!"

"I won't," Carlene vowed, then she smiled wistfully. "It's so romantic, Kelly-Ann. You'll see. Steve won't disappoint you. He's a romantic at heart, honest."

Kelly-Ann gazed at the younger woman. She wasn't naive enough to allow herself to believe a young girl with a starry look in her eyes. She couldn't bear to believe Steve cared if it wasn't true. Steve Jamison probably wouldn't return. She and Carlene were both going to be disappointed.

She didn't know why the thought hurt so much. She hadn't expected to see him again anyway, had she?

And she certainly shouldn't be sitting here discussing her poor heart's innermost secrets with the man's sister!

Chapter Thirteen

Kelly-Ann managed to change the subject. She and Carlene were eating chips and salsa and drinking ice tea while they talked about animals when Steve bounded back into the restaurant, his hair disheveled, his tie off to one side, his face red.

"Janet must have given him a rough time," Kelly-Ann murmured, watching as Steve approached the table at a more leisurely pace than he'd entered the building.

"Huh!" Carlene grunted. "He didn't stick around for Janet to do *anything*. He looks like that only when he's in an awful rush, and that's not often, I can tell you."

Green eyes widening, Kelly-Ann told herself she could testify to Steve's whirlwind appearance. He looked as he had the first time she saw him, only he'd had on mismatched clothes then.

"Hi," he said warmly, taking a chair beside Kelly-Ann, instead of sitting in the booth beside his sister. "I hope you two went ahead and ordered."

He was smiling broadly, and Kelly-Ann hated what her insides were doing. He kept looking at her as if he'd been dying to see her. His gorgeous brown eyes were dancing, and his full mouth seemed to have a permanent smile.

"We waited for you," Carlene said.

"Then let's order," he insisted. "You shouldn't have waited." He motioned to a waiter, then turned to Kelly-Ann. "Is that salsa too hot for you?"

"No," she murmured, wondering how he could sit there beside her so close and act as if this were the most normal situation in the world.

"How did you two happen to come here?" he asked, still looking at Kelly-Ann.

She wasn't even sure he'd heard her answer about the sauce. Clearly he had something on his mind and wanted to get to it. She didn't know if she wanted him to or not.

"I called and asked Kelly-Ann if I could work in her shop," Carlene answered blithely. "I've decided what I'm going to be, Steve," she continued enthusiastically. "I'm going to train exotic animals."

Both Kelly-Ann and Steve looked at the girl, then at each other. "It's news to me, too," Kelly-Ann said when Steve frowned. "I didn't make the decision."

"I made it all by myself," Carlene announced proudly. She leaned forward, almost putting her hand in the salsa. "Steve, can I please bring Kelly-Ann's parrot to the condo? I can start to work with him. Kelly-Ann says he's been abused and needs lots of care and attention."

"You're kidding!" Steve said.

Carlene shook her head. "No, he's been abused—"

"I don't mean you're kidding about his condition," Steve exclaimed. "I mean you *have* to be kidding about wanting to bring him into my home!"

Carlene looked as though she might cry. "You don't have to be hateful about it, Steve," the girl said. "He needs me, and I need him. I can't take him back to school, and you know it."

"I . . ." Steve turned to Kelly-Ann.

"Not guilty!" she cried. "All I did was introduce Carlene to my animals."

He faced his sister again. "What about Jeffy and the commercial prospects? What about going to California this summer?"

"Oh, I still plan to go," Carlene said. "That's what helped me decide on a career. I've worked with the handler and Jeffy for weeks now, and I'm good with him."

"You are," Steve agreed.

"In fact," Carlene said proudly, "even the trainer says I'm a natural. And when I saw that Amazon parrot at Kelly-Ann's house, well it hit me! I want to be an animal trainer."

"Carlene, you know so little about animals," Steve said practically. "Jeffy is literally the first pet you've ever had. Isn't this a sudden decision?"

"No!" Carlene protested. "It isn't my fault Mother and Father used an excuse to put me in a boarding school and not let me have a pet. Oh, please, don't be selfish and self-centered, Steve," she pleaded as if her very life depended on it. "Kelly-Ann is going to let me work half a day on Saturdays so I can get some experience. Please don't ruin my whole life by refusing to let me have the parrot.''

Selfish and self-centered. That's what Kelly-Ann had once said about him. If he didn't know better, he'd think the two of them had plotted against him.

He looked at Kelly-Ann. He *did* know better. He was the first to admit that Carlene could manipulate him, but it wasn't in Kelly-Ann. She was the only woman he'd ever met who was simply what she appeared to be.

She looked bewildered. She hadn't anticipated any of this. ''The parrot can stay at my house and still be Carlene's if that's all right with everyone,'' she murmured, not finding it totally satisfactory herself, but hoping it would ease the tension.

Steve looked back at his sister. ''Let's eat dinner and think on it.''

''Oh, Steve!'' Carlene protested. ''Don't be like Daddy!''

''Carlene,'' he cautioned.

She turned to Kelly-Ann. ''May I come and live with you, Kelly-Ann? My family doesn't care about me, and you have plenty of room.''

''Carlene!'' both Steve and Kelly-Ann said.

''That's not fair, and it's not true,'' Steve said.

He honestly didn't know how he'd gotten in this mess, and he had no idea how he would get out of it. However, he did know, suddenly, how much he would miss Carlene when she was no longer there to come home to. He'd grown used to her chatter, her company, even her complaints, and he cared that she was unhappy.

He looked at Kelly-Ann again. ''Will you go out with me on Friday? You and I can talk about it then, without Carlene, who's clearly too emotional at the moment.''

"Steve," his sister said, "*that's* not fair. It's one thing to be shuffled off to school without having any say-so, but you and Kelly-Ann can't decide whether or not I get the bird. That's between you and me, since she's planning to give the bird away." Staring at her brother intently, she said, "Don't use me as an excuse to see her again. Find your own!"

Kelly-Ann looked at Steve and suddenly felt sorry for him. Clearly Carlene was more than he'd bargained for.

He looked uncomfortable, but he met the teenager's eyes. "You're absolutely right, and I bow to your viewpoint. You and I will discuss whether or not you get the bird when we get home."

He turned to Kelly-Ann. "Will you join me Friday night? I know a great place in Greensboro with a superior dance band. You do dance, don't you?" he added, finding the idea that she might not inconceivable. She was so full of life.

"Yes, I enjoy dancing," she said, thoroughly flustered, "but, Steve, you don't have to take me out. We can discuss this—"

He shook his head. "Carlene's right, Kelly-Ann. I *was* using her as an excuse because I didn't know what else to do. I want to be with you. I've wanted that for two weeks, and she's also right that I've been self-centered and nasty, but *that's* something you and I need to discuss alone."

Kelly-Ann despised the way her insides turned topsy-turvy. Was Carlene also right about the other things she'd said? Kelly-Ann was too afraid to dream it was true, although she wasn't about to turn down the date—just in case this Piscean man was all she'd imagined he might be.

"Yes," she agreed. "I'd love to go dancing."

"Good," he said, managing a smile for her, even though he thought these women might drive him to an early grave.

"Well, I'm glad we got that mess straightened out," Carlene said. "You and Kelly-Ann are wasting time. Life's too short to throw away good times."

Steve and Kelly-Ann looked at each other again. Kelly-Ann was on pins and needles, wondering if the girl knew what she was talking about.

Steve couldn't deny what his sister said. "Out of the mouths of babes..." he murmured.

The waiter cleared his throat. None of them seemed to realize he was standing beside them. "Are you ready to order, *señor,* and *señoritas?*" he asked.

When they had placed their orders, Steve turned back to Kelly-Ann again. "I don't know about you, but I have to thank my sister for her input this evening, and for bringing you."

Warmth rushed through Kelly-Ann. She laughed nervously. "Why, thank you, Steve. I really didn't know you were going to be here."

He smiled. "I'm sure you didn't."

Carlene stretched out against the back of the booth, her ire departing as quickly as it had come. "And I must thank you for giving me credit," she said. "Cupid and me. Now can I have the bird?"

Steve tossed a tortilla chip at her. Carlene giggled, caught it and put it into her purse.

"What are you doing?" he asked.

"It's for the parrot," she said. "I know you're going to let me have him."

When Steve shook his head, Kelly-Ann watched the interplay between brother and sister with interest. The evening had been most informative. She could only wonder what Friday would bring!

When Steve arrived Friday night, a nervous Kelly-Ann invited him into the house. No matter how many times she'd told her heart to be still, it had soared through the day in anticipation of this evening.

"You look lovely," Steve murmured, his eyes alone nearly seducing her with their dark, hungry look.

Kelly-Ann glanced down at the flowered formfitting dress she'd worn. True, she'd purchased it with the pure, unadulterated intention of luring Steve Jamison into loving her. But the way he was looking at her now made her wonder if perhaps she'd overdone it.

"Is it really all right?" she asked hesitantly. The clerk who sold it to her had said she was a man killer in it. Still . . .

Steve laughed and drew her into his arms. "Your naiveté about your incredibly sensual beauty makes you all the more adorable," he said. "The dress isn't 'all right'—it's gorgeous. And you're gorgeous in it. You look absolutely ravishing."

She smiled, still a little nervous. "You do, too," she said blatantly. "I've never seen you look so sexy, and I remember how sexy I thought you were the very first . . ."

Her words trailed off. She was moving way too fast here. "I really do like your suit," she said simply.

He looked at it. "I picked it out myself, just for you," he admitted. "Is it really all right? I stuck with dark colors, knowing pale ones aren't my forte."

They both laughed. "You look wonderful," she said sincerely.

"Well, I didn't dare ask Carlene," he joked. "My sister has made me realize I'm not as self-sufficient as I thought, that my world isn't as perfectly laid out as I imagined." He grinned. "I don't know whether I was due the comeuppance or if Carlene just knows how to pull my strings."

Kelly-Ann smiled. "Does that mean she gets the parrot?"

Laughing openly, Steve nodded. "She put me on a guilt trip, of course. If she really thinks she wants to work with exotic animals, I believe she should be given the chance."

Kelly-Ann was only a little surprised. More and more, she had been getting glimpses of the famous Piscean sensitivity. "So you're going to let her have the bird?" she pressed.

"Conditionally," he answered. "If you'll help me out. Kelly-Ann, I can't keep that bird in the building, but if you'll let him stay at your house so that she can work with him on weekends, I'd be indebted to you forever."

Forever, she thought, her heart soaring.

"Kelly-Ann?" he prompted. "I know you hoped to give him a permanent home. However, this is a compromise that may work for all three of us."

She nodded. "I don't know about you, Steve, but it seems to me that compromises are a way of life. I don't mind at all. I'm kind of used to the bird anyway."

He looked at her; their gazes locked. Kelly-Ann swallowed and mustered the courage to say something that had been on her mind for several days.

"Steve, do you really think I'm a bad neighbor?" she asked anxiously. "I don't want to be a bad neighbor and I didn't think I was, not even when you called and said that. But I realize everyone isn't on my wavelength and that animals aren't everyone's priority, and I understand why," she quickly added.

Steve smiled. "Everyone may not be on your wavelength, but I find myself on it more and more. I'm sorry I was so harsh with you on the phone. That just goes to show what people will do and say when they don't know the other side of the story."

"You don't need to apologize," she said. "I truly thought I had every right to let the animals live here. After all, I was in this neighborhood first," she said. "Now I don't know what to think anymore."

"Can't the shelter handle them?" Steve asked, trying to think of a solution.

"They're overbooked as it is," she said. "Anyway, I can't give up my pets, Steve. They're my family. I love them. I don't think you understand how deeply."

He smiled, but he wondered if he did understand. "We'll think of something. At least, I hope we will," he amended, the enormity of the endless lines of homeless pets coming in and out of this house almost overwhelming.

Kelly-Ann noticed that Steve was starting to drift again. The playfulness about their attire had disappeared, and he was frowning.

She was determined to confront this problem head-on.

"Steve, tell me why you can't make a statement and stick with it. You always vacillate. Well, almost always," she said. "And you have these most disturbing mood swings that I find terribly difficult to deal with."

Steve looked surprised. "So do you!" he insisted.
"In fact, if you'll remember, you drove me crazy at
lunch on our very first day together!"

She looked stunned. "I knew I'd picked up some of
your traits," she said, "but I didn't realize how it
seemed when I couldn't make up my mind about what
to do. Especially what to do about you," she said.

"Kelly-Ann," he murmured, "the mood swings and
vacillation aren't a real problem." His eyes burned
brightly. "Since the moment I first saw you, I've been
afraid—afraid of this dynamite attraction I feel toward you. I simply didn't know what to do!"

"Steve!" Kelly-Ann cried. She'd felt the very same
way, of course! She knew it was madness, yet for her
it truly had been love at first sight.

He held up his hand. "Let me finish while I can still
think somewhat coherently. Things happened too
fast," he said. "I'm a little gun shy—or I was—about
marriage. I want it to last forever. Like you, I don't
want to go into it with any other conditions except love,
and I am in love with you, Kelly-Ann Keernan."

"Steve, I—"

"Wait, please," he said again. "I need to finish. I
know it sounds like love at first sight and all kinds of
other flights of fantasy, but it's been weeks now, and I
can't get you out of my mind. I even wanted to take
that damned parrot home myself, just to please you.
And," he added truthfully, "because he fascinated
me."

He held one of her hands to his lips and kissed it.
"*You* fascinate me. I've never met anyone like you, you
with your sun signs and animals and warmth and
beauty."

"Oh, Steve," she breathed.

Suddenly the piercing ring of the phone shattered the romantic moment. The couple stared at each other.

"Maybe it will quit," Steve murmured. "I'm not through talking to you, Kelly-Ann."

She nodded, wishing the discordant clatter had never intruded, but she couldn't ignore it.

"Maybe it's important," she said, when it continued to ring so insistently.

Steve sighed. "If you're going to answer, please make it quick."

Nodding, Kelly-Ann jerked up the receiver. Hearing Steve's frantic sister on the other end, she handed the phone to him. "It's Carlene. Jeffy's lost."

"Lost?" he repeated. Then he tried to calm the teenager.

Seconds later, he hung up. "I'm so sorry, but I've got to rush back home. Carlene is nearly hysterical. It seems that one of the men who lives in the building— the one who always complains about your pets, in fact—has deliberately let Jeffy out of the backyard. Carlene is beside herself."

His eyes met Kelly-Ann's. "And I'm pretty damned upset myself."

"I'll go with you," she said, quickly grabbing up her purse.

When they reached the condo, Carlene was frantic. "Mr. Wicker did it!" she cried the moment her brother entered the backyard. "I heard Jeffy barking, and when I went to check on him, I saw Mr. Wicker walking away from our gate. It was standing wide open! I swear it, Steve. And I can't find Jeffy anywhere. I've called and I've looked."

Kelly-Ann and Steve stared sympathetically at the weeping girl, who was shining a flashlight all around the forested area that surrounded the condominium complex.

"He's never been out by himself," she sobbed.

Steve pulled her into his arms. "Shh. Calm down. We'll find him. He can't have gone far."

Carlene looked at Steve with big tearful eyes. "Jeffy's the only thing in the world that was ever mine, that ever loved me as much as I loved him without nagging at me or complaining or getting hateful with me."

"Unconditional love," Steve murmured almost subconsciously. "I understand, sweetheart, and we're going to find him. Let me go inside and get another flashlight."

Kelly-Ann didn't wait for Steve to return. She knew the woods around the condos. She'd played all over this area as a young child, and she knew secret places and small animal burrows that might entice a young dog with a big taste of first-time freedom.

With Carlene right behind her, she started toward the stream down at the bottom of the hill. Steve caught up with them in seconds. All three of them were calling Jeffy's name, but it was, ironically, Steve, not Carlene or Kelly-Ann who found him, although Kelly-Ann had pointed them in the right direction.

Suddenly, Jeffy jumped up out of the darkness, his muddy paws on Steve's chest, his breathing hard. Before Steve could grab him, he jumped back down and started running all around the bushes and trees again.

"George Washington Jefferson IV, come here this instant!" Carlene ordered. Then, when the dog didn't obey, she gathered her wits about her, shined her light on him and commanded, "Sit, Jeffy!"

The collie immediately sat down in the grass, his mouth hanging open as though he was grinning at them for having pulled off such a stunt.

Everyone breathed a sigh of relief when Carlene walked over to the dog and attached his collar to a leash.

Laughing through her tears, Carlene turned to her brother and hugged him. "I was so scared, Steve. You have no idea how scared I was."

He tilted her chin. "I have an idea, Kitten. You take Jeffy on back to the house. Kelly-Ann and I will be there in a few minutes, and don't you worry about Mr. Wicker. I'll deal with him myself."

When Carlene had walked away with Jeffy, Steve looped arms with Kelly-Ann, and they began to walk back toward the condos.

"I do have an idea how scared Carlene was," he said, sounding amazed. "I was scared, too, not just for Carlene and Jeffy, but for myself, as well. I hadn't realized how attached I'd gotten to him."

Kelly-Ann smiled. "I knew you had a world of love inside that supposedly rigid and orderly life when you tried to rescue my fish from my cat," she teased. "It just took something like this to make you realize how much you cared."

He stopped and drew her against him. "It took something like dinner at the Mexican restaurant and Carlene's observations to make me realize how much I love you," he said solemnly. "Now I need to know where that leaves me. When Carlene called, I think we were at the part about me loving you, but how do you feel?"

Even in the dark of the night, Kelly-Ann could see his anticipation, his doubt, his need. She wanted to quickly reassure him that he couldn't possibly care for her any more than she did him.

"I was getting ready to tell you, Steve," she said, "that I fell in love with you the moment you raced into the shop that very first day."

"Kelly-Ann, now don't say something—"

"It's true," she said holding her fingers to his lips to silence him. "But I didn't believe you could love me. We started off on the wrong foot, and I thought you'd be mad at me forever."

"Kelly-Ann . . ." he began again.

She silenced him again. "My turn," she said. "I was pleased and surprised when you came back, then I was confused and uncertain. I thought you wanted someone much more sophisticated, someone like Suzette, someone who would fit better into your life. Or worse, I thought you didn't want to get married, and you know I want babies. . . ."

She let the word trail off. Did Steve want children? What if he didn't?

Steve laughed. "I *know* you want babies! I asked you how many a couple of times."

She remembered. He had asked her, and she'd decided it was none of his business.

"Seven," she said breathlessly, "though I want to adopt some of them. There are so many children out there. . . ." Her words trailed off again, and she blushed furiously.

Steve stared at her. Seven!

"Why seven?" he finally managed to ask.

She shrugged and smiled sheepishly. "Seven is a lucky number, and anyway, I already have seven pets for the children, and . . ." She let her words fade away again.

"Ah, Kelly-Ann Keernan," Steve said, "you might as well say it all and get it over with. You're the woman I want. I have to know it all. I've been fighting the attraction, the love, with everything in me. I knew it even before Carlene told me to find my own excuse to see you again."

"What about the way I live, Steve?" she whispered, not wanting the dream to get away. "What about my animals? What about my babies?"

He smiled. "What about them? I think tonight was my final lesson in how important creatures are—people and animals. I've been headed in that direction since Jeffy and Carlene came to live with me. But we'll have to get a larger place, of course."

He tried to see her expression in the faint light of the moon. "I wonder how you would feel about having Carlene and Jeffy live with us, too. After all, she only has two years of school left—"

"I'd love it!" she exclaimed.

Steve gazed adoringly at her. "You really would, wouldn't you? You wouldn't mind at all sharing yourself with a teenage girl who's a bit troubled and a dog who's more than a little spoiled...and a man who still has lessons to learn about what's important in life, would you?"

Kelly-Ann smiled sweetly. "All of us learn lessons all the time. Life is a lesson, Steve, right down from the color blindness and cowlick over which you have no control, to who comes in and out of our lives."

Steve drew her tightly to him. "And I thank God, fate, the stars, whomever, that you came into my life, Kelly-Ann Keernan. You will marry me, won't you?" He lightly brushed her lips with his. "After all, you yourself told me to take the first caring person I met the day of the dog show. That's you," he said with a big grin.

"Yes, I'll marry you!" she cried. She could feel her face turning red. "You know, Steve, it was all meant to be. You and I were matched up long before we ever met."

"Of course, I know," he said, only half teasing. "I knew that from the moment I saw your home, the love you have for your animals, the cats in rocking chairs in Shop Number One."

Kelly-Ann blushed. "Suzette specifically asked me not to put rocking chairs in the other shop."

He smiled. "What sign is she?"

Both of them laughed again. Then Steve murmured, "I want to spend every day with you for the rest of our lives."

"Oh, Steve," she whispered, "I promise I'll love you forever."

"And I you," he vowed.

Their lips met and sealed their promise of love, their vow of forever, their destiny.

* * * * *

MORE ABOUT
THE PISCES MAN

by Lydia Lee

If you're looking for romance par excellence, look no farther than the Neptune-ruled Pisces man: he fairly breathes it. Frequently he'll have a poetic nature and he'll be wining and dining you all the time. His is a gentle, psychic and slightly dreamy nature and he incorporates the strengths and weaknesses of the other eleven signs. For example, despite his nebulous nature, he can tackle a Virgoan job with amazing organization, then turn around and wow you with the wit of a Gemini. Although you might not know it, under that deceptively placid exterior lies a man with the power and sensuality of a Scorpio. There's only one small hitch. This man often doesn't have any idea how very special he really is. At this point you're probably wondering what his weaknesses are. He's got them, but don't worry. You'll hardly notice his flaws because you'll be too busy enjoying life through rose-colored glasses with this visionary. He'll undoubtedly have a handle on reality, and he'll also have an almost magical ability to manifest his dreams. Of course, you have to also understand that if he's busy writing the great American novel he might not have time to tend to earthier matters, like getting bills paid on time. Heaven forbid that you, his lady fair, should criticize him. His feelings will get hurt and he might swim away until the tempest is over. There's not a lot you can do about that, except avoid carping!

Did you ever try to catch a fish with your hands? Slippery little devils, aren't they? In fact, about the best advice when dealing with the Neptune-ruled man is to forget about pinning him down. You have to charm him slowly. Step into his magical dance; even bolster his ego occasionally. He will respond in kind. Remember, this man literally wrote the book on love and magic.

Pisces run the gamut of humanity: everything from saint to swindler. There are basically two types of fish—one going upstream and one going downstream. The latter, unfortunately, often lose themselves in illusion. Somewhere along the line, their compassion and understanding for the rest of mankind may get twisted and turn into self-pity. Or maybe they didn't fashion their tools to deal with the real world. Their deceptions, when they stoop that low, are so clever that even they are fooled!

Luckily for Pisces, the universe seems to give them extra chances. In its wisdom, it knows they're more than capable of pulling themselves out of the swamp and swimming with the best of them—upstream.

This is Pisces' challenge, to go against the tide, to find their strengths and leave the world a richer place for their talents. This water sign has talents for just about everything, including romance. Falling in love with the mystical fish can be an exhilarating experience for even the most jaded woman. He'll take you places you've never been before, or he'll describe them so well you'll feel you've been there. If he's one of the upstream fishes, that promise of travel could materialize into a yacht trip around the world, for these men love to travel. Don't go anyplace too tawdry or depressing, however, for Pisces men soak things up like sponges and depression is truly their nemesis. Keep their surroundings cheerful and upbeat and you'll have a happy Pisces man to accompany you through life.

If you're interested in meeting one of these special men you might try your local art gallery, the movies, church, little theater or a nice ocean voyage. You'll recognize him by bedroom eyes that suggest pleasures to rival a thousand and one nights. With all that magic at his disposal, it just keeps getting better.

*　*　*　*　*

Famous Pisces Men

George Harrison
Rudolf Nureyev
Enrico Caruso
Johnny Cash
Frederic Chopin
Michelangelo

Silhouette Romance®

LONG, TALL TEXANS

HARDEN
Diana Palmer

In her bestselling LONG, TALL TEXANS series, Diana Palmer brought you to Jacobsville and introduced you to the rough and rugged ranchers who call the town home. Now, hot and dusty Jacobsville promises to get even hotter when hard-hearted, woman-hating rancher Harden Tremayne has to reckon with the lovely Miranda Warren.

The LONG, TALL TEXANS series continues! Don't miss HARDEN by Diana Palmer in March . . . only from Silhouette Romance.

LTT-1

SILHOUETTE'S "BIG WIN"
SWEEPSTAKES RULES & REGULATIONS

NO PURCHASE NECESSARY TO ENTER OR RECEIVE A PRIZE

1. To enter the Sweepstakes and join the Reader Service, scratch off the metallic strips on all your BIG WIN tickets #1-#6. This will reveal the potential values for each Sweepstakes entry number, the number of free book(s) you will receive and your free bonus gift as part of our Reader Service. If you do not wish to take advantage of our Reader Service but wish to enter the Sweepstakes only, scratch off the metallic strips on your BIG WIN tickets #1-#4. Return your entire sheet of tickets intact. Incomplete and/or inaccurate entries are ineligible for that section or sections of prizes. Torstar Corp. and its affiliates are not responsible for mutilated or unreadable entries or inadvertent printing errors. Mechanically reproduced entries are null and void.

2. Whether you take advantage of this offer or not, on or about April 30, 1992, at the offices of Marden-Kane Inc., Lake Success, NY, your Sweepstakes numbers will be compared against the list of winning numbers generated at random by the computer. However, prizes will only be awarded to individuals who have entered the Sweepstakes. In the event that all prizes are not claimed, a random drawing will be held from all qualified entries received from March 30, 1990 to March 31, 1992, to award all unclaimed prizes. All cash prizes (Grand to Sixth), will be mailed to the winners and are payable by check in U.S. funds. Seventh prize will be shipped to winners via third-class mail. These prizes are in addition to any free, surprise or mystery gifts that might be offered. Versions of this Sweepstakes with different prizes of approximate equal value may appear at retail outlets or in other mailings by Torstar Corp. and its affiliates.

3. The following prizes are awarded in this sweepstakes: ★ Grand Prize (1) $1,000,000; First Prize (1) $25,000; Second Prize (1) $10,000; Third Prize (5) $5,000; Fourth Prize (10) $1,000; Fifth Prize (100) $250; Sixth Prize (2,500) $10; ★ ★ Seventh Prize (6,000) $12.95 ARV.

   ★ This presentation offers a Grand Prize of a $1,000,000 annuity. Winner will receive $33,333.33 a year for 30 years without interest totalling $1,000,000.

   ★ ★ Seventh Prize: A fully illustrated hardcover book published by Torstar Corp. Approximate Retail Value of the book is $12.95.

   Entrants may cancel the Reader Service at anytime without cost or obligation to buy (see details in center insert card).

4. This Sweepstakes is being conducted under the supervision of an independent judging organization. By entering this Sweepstakes, each entrant accepts and agrees to be bound by these rules and the decisions of the judges, which shall be final and binding. Odds of winning in the random drawing are dependent upon the total number of entries received. Taxes, if any, are the sole responsibility of the winners. Prizes are nontransferable. All entries must be received at the address printed on the reply card and must be postmarked no later than 12:00 MIDNIGHT on March 31, 1992. The drawing for all unclaimed Sweepstakes prizes will take place on May 30, 1992, at 12:00 NOON, at the offices of Marden-Kane, Inc., Lake Success, New York.

5. This offer is open to residents of the U.S., the United Kingdom, France and Canada, 18 years or older, except employees and their immediate family members of Torstar Corp., its affiliates, subsidiaries, and all the other agencies, entities and persons connected with the use, marketing or conduct of this Sweepstakes. All Federal, State, Provincial and local laws apply. Void wherever prohibited or restricted by law. Any litigation within the Province of Quebec respecting the conduct and awarding of a prize in this publicity contest must be submitted to the Régie des Loteries et Courses du Québec.

6. Winners will be notified by mail and may be required to execute an affidavit of eligibility and release, which must be returned within 14 days after notification or an alternate winner will be selected. Canadian winners will be required to correctly answer an arithmetical skill-testing question administered by mail, which must be returned within a limited time. Winners consent to the use of their names, photographs and/or likenesses for advertising and publicity in conjunction with this and similar promotions without additional compensation. For a list of our major prize winners, send a stamped, self-addressed ENVELOPE to: WINNERS LIST, c/o Marden-Kane Inc., P.O. Box 701, SAYREVILLE, NJ 08871. Requests for Winners Lists will be fulfilled after the May 30, 1992 drawing date.

If Sweepstakes entry form is missing, please print your name and address on a 3" × 5" piece of plain paper and send to:

In the U.S.
Silhouette's "BIG WIN" Sweepstakes
3010 Walden Ave.
P.O. Box 1867
Buffalo, NY 14269-1867

In Canada
Silhouette's "BIG WIN" Sweepstakes
P.O. Box 609
Fort Erie, Ontario
L2A 5X3

Offer limited to one per household.

LTY-S391D